TZVI's TREEs

Original Stories About Weed

TZVI PECKAR the THIRD

•*a POLYMORPH productions PUBLICATION*•

DEDICATED TO
Jerome
& all his Good Dogs n' BBQ Ribs

TZVI's TREEs

Original Stories About Weed

.:WARNING:.
DO NOT ASH ON THIS BOOK
PAGES ARE HIGHLY FLAMAMBLE

#01
PRIMO

"Live your life," he says.

"I don't know what that means, bro?"

"Means, what it means," is philosophy in a nutshell for this guy I've known for six or so years, one of my friends, a friend's friend, but I've known this twig of a Neo-Los Angeles-Hippie long enough to consider him a friend. He sits shotgun, sips on the freshly sparked jay, as we pull into a warehouse parking lot. "Hey, Kev, pass it, don't burn it," I say as I repeatedly clamp my finger and thumb. He takes another sip, I clamp at him a couple more times. I know the breeze of the convertible is going to mess up the burn. Sip, sip. Kev passes the joint back. It's boating. I lick my fingers, slow the burn. "Boated," I tell him. Kev ignores me, coughs, gives the driver directions, I'm not that aware. The joint's still burning wrong. Sucks. I lick my fingertips again, dap, dap, slow the burn, slow, burn, slow, good puppy. Puff it into a steady...BUMP...speed bumps jolt our '72 Dodge convertible, and the jay boat's cherry has popped out, landed on the upholstery. I swipe it to the floor. There's a fresh burn hole in the seat, I tap out the simmering cherry of weed on the floor. Nobody saw nothing.

"Doesn't this car use a lot of gas for LA?" I ask.

"All my grandfather left me," says the fat man behind the wheel, our driver.

"I'm sorry to hear that," I pass the joint back to Kev.

"What happened?" Kev examines the boated burnt paper.

*

The sun'll come up in about an hour or so, I figure. The Dodge rolls over yet another speed bump and Kev points out the last parking spot in the lot, "Way down there, kill the lights."

"Anybody actually around?" I ask Kev.

"Bugs," he says.

"Cops?" I ask, "FBI?"

"No dude, bugs. Buzz, buzz..." Kev says, shaking his head at Aton, "Mosquitos."

"In LA?"

"LA river's right there," Kev motions toward the tree line on the opposite side of the lot fence. Thud, speed bump, Thud, Thud, two in a row. Over kill. Aton cuts the lights a few yards before the spot and rolls in, shuts the motor, and Kev throws his arm over the seat, looks me right in the eye, clears his throat and insists, "Do not tell them you're from Jamaica."

"I'm not," I remind him for the eight hundredth time.

"Dude, you're fucking Jamaican," he believes his own anything.

"I was raised in the Keys, not Jamaica. The Keys are in America. My parents are Jamaican, but I'm American," but Aton interrupts me.

"Dude, you're Jamaican?" he asks.

"See? That's why I don't want you saying nothing in there," Kev has found his burden of proof, and that's it, that's all the instruction bro's got for me, car door opens, Kev's out, door closes, Aton looks at me, "Gonna be dope. Ya man?"

Sometimes I think I'm alone in my ambivalence about weed culture. Aton is so impressed with the Hydroponic setup, Kev's like a dictionary of strain knowledge, and maybe that's why they don't want me to say anything about my heritage? I've smoked since sixteen, but I don't know, I'm not a connoisseur, like, that would be religious, and I'm not into that—"You grow inside 'cause LA's so smoggy?" I ask Kev.

"This is primo shit, man," he boasts, "Smog don't get in here, see," and points out the ventilation system. The tubes and fans look complex; the duct tape makes me wonder. Kev pulls down a branch from a budding plant, right into my nose, the kief sprinkles off onto my goatee, does smell great, I sneeze, apologize, then simply ask the owner—

"I don't get it. Looks more designer than Primo. Shouldn't primo plant life be found in the wild, totally free from anything that would impede its natural growth; a specifically designed place on the earth just for marijuana, because the elements lined up perfectly in that spot and nowhere else is as 'Primo' to grow naturally? A plot of soil sitting in the most opportune place for sunlight on a time schedule for the plant to flourish, and the precise amount of clean rain, maybe a small stream the keeps the roots tender and happy? A fine balance of moisture to dryness in the air per day—and a perfect natural selection of plants and animals that would protect the plant from infestation. This place would be beautiful. The plant would grow in nature's bliss, and we would call it a miracle, and that miracle would deserve the title: Primo Shit."

"Damn," the grower is impressed, pats Kev on the back, "You were right, this guy's pure Jamaican," and Kev smiles at me, but I'm not complaining, these gentlemen hooked up the Jamaican from the Keys and I left with a pound of LA side river warehouse primo bud 'cause he didn't want any bad juju on his grow house—~*
The end.

02

LIFE

BEES

My intentions were good, she was beautiful, a virgin for sure. The males had been banished months ago. Pure. Her aroma was strong, radial, a powder thick smell. I was across the river the size of a creek, as deep as the sea. They had told me I shouldn't be here. Said it was a curse beyond mortality. The pleasures were too great. Men lost to the bottom of the river. The current pulls a man under, not down like the rivers of the mountains. This river ran on leveled ground, curled along the valley and then back again. A small path of wetlands that leads to the meadow between the two rivers; waterways that are one in the same. Prior to my arrival at this natural beauty, I had shot the bar stools who had volunteered unwanted pessimism. I had come to this corner of the earth to mate my wife, not drown in the waters of scavengers and connoisseurs. There has never been a creature more majestic as she.

I know from the tales, the myths, the glorified lies perpetrated by the locals to keep the hoarders away that my presence is an annoyance. I am the ultimate hoarder, yet I only desire to hoard one thing in this short lifetime, her, and all the love she has to give to me. This female of the soil deserves to be treated as a treasure; she is to be loved as a living soul. I fingered the ring in my pocket. My mate has not been born from the rib of man; my mate has birthed from seed.

*

"I am not a visitor!"
I exclaim my presence from across the water. Her decorative locks drift in the breeze; leaves, feathers from the stalk, so massive they collect and consciously distribute the rain to her roots. I know she knows of me. How could she not? Hasn't she been in-waiting for my shears? Shears that I will use to cut pieces of her love in order for me to take my time as I enjoy her flesh. It is moments before mid-day. I am no fool. I will have my wife. I will be as cunning as a fox who strategizes a solemn plan to arrive at the very moment that the environment has its guard down, as it focuses on its hunger...the rain.

*

I have approached her back. She has no front, no sides. She is complete from top to bottom. Her arms, feathers, flesh, all have sprouted from along her spine, her stalk, whose legs are but a million strands of hair dug into the depths of the soil, matted, knotted, coiled together fabricating a woven nest grappling dirt and stone. Even from the distance of a foot or two, you can make out her exposed nerves; her transparent red hairs, red strands twisting out from the blades of her thick green leaves.

"I love you," I whisper. A breath of voice caught in the wind, blown closer to her essence.

"I am breath underwater," she replies.

"Yes," I think, "No, you are above the ground, higher ground. Higher than that of the sea," I say, "You are the love of my existence, and I have come so far, only to be with you," and she stands, a storm cloud of denial and distortion cover the sun above the rivers. She has grown angry. She desires only to drink; waters from the rivers, moister from the heavens. She rather I leave her be. I rather set our love on fire— and this she knows.

The chase is on. I will love

the female grown from soil.

She has, with the ease of miracles, uprooted herself from the moist earth— throwing stones, catapulted from the force of her roots as they tear themselves from the ground. I am aim. One after another, pelted by the rocks. Far from a biblical stoning, I have done nothing, but sniffed her sent as it permeated the air, and sprinkled particles of golden dry sift into my face as she ran to cross the river   *

                                                  *

                        I've swam rivers filled with drowning honey bees,
                    I've swallowed minnows from the bellies of toads,
I've kept catfish alive w/ the tail of a scoundrel,

*   If I chase the broken willows to the ends of the earth,*

If I felt the insatiable drift of rivers into her seas,
                If I conned every one of them to feast in the flames?
                                Would I be here, as I could have been there?

                                                  *

                                                                      *

She skips so easily to the opposing shore; as for me, I stumble, I fall, I am soaked, but not yet have I drowned. Waist deep, my toe balanced upon a single stone, small, no larger than the pebble you'd find washed ashore, I call out to her, "If not I, then what purpose must you have to blossom?" She halts her retreat towards the woods — and I continue...

"Without a reason, you live only to die. Isn't that your purpose?"

No more than a moment had to pass before she turned away again, and again I knew no front nor side, but she turned and said to my back, with a grin that I imagined a rack of golden kiefed grills, "You have played yourself a fool, fool."

I step ashore.

"Love is the only use of a fool," I step, she stays, I step, she stays, her roots digging back into the soil.

"I live to be ingested," she whispers, her leaves spread apart from her sensual buds, microscopically fleshy tentacles, that of a sea urchin, what one imagines in the depths of the female ocean, a living tingler, one for the mind.

"Beautiful," I whisper.

"Cold," she whimpers.

"Fire," and I spark my lighter, snip her stalk, discard her spine, and make my return to the cities, towns, alleys, embankments, stock markets, and rallies. Clone her once, and you've cloned her again and again. Then they'll make mutts out of her, all baring my name, our marriage in discovery. And then I was robbed. Her essence, fragrance, bastard seeds, all gone in a swift night. Stolen by the best, my own insatiable need to keep her around...without a care in the world.

#03
DROPPI N'BUD(s)

I swear I had a good grip on that little nugget. I had my index on the stem and my thumb on the head, glitter and golden, two untrimmed purple leaves popping out like Dumbo ears, and poof.

Gone— just like that — poof.

I didn't hear it hit the floor. There was no bounce—The bud so light the air ate all its sound away— poof.

*

When I moved into this place, it was, *"alright,"* but what really sold me on this half-room of an apartment was the green fluffed up carpet.

The few footsteps it took to make your way across the stay, barefoot, felt like walking on the softest grass, a moss, but sturdy, always bounced back. Warm too. You don't want wooden floors up here. Alaska's carpet necessary, but as of now, tonight, dropping the bud, for the second time this week— well the aesthetic of my green grass has lost out to practicality.

I <u>need</u> to find the nugget.

What's this?

A dust bunny?

...but it's firm, has bulk, there's something in there. I got to sit down. Take my time to examine this. Light is bad in here.

Desk lamp, in the bathroom. Hate missing. Rather see in there, then...I cross my legs, American Indian style. Om— Wrong tribe. I'm so stoned. No. Not true. Not stoned enough. When I find the bud, maybe both of those runaways, I can smoke 'em, even though I made myself a promise.

One bud at a time, that's my pact to stability, conscientiousness, modularity, what's the word, tip of my tongue— MODERATION...because I have a fucking mountain of weed on this collapsed dining table. I get up, sit on my single bed. Examine this duster ball, make sure it's not the snowballed static electricity of my precious first bed of the beast. I could call it in. Not get too deep into a missing persons case on my own. I'm no detective. Call it in.

Amber Alert
Lost Nugget.
Green.
.02 grams.
Red Hairs, purple Ears; speaks English and Mexican —
Answers to the name Kushy Kush-Kush.

*

"Dusty, you gonna help me find Kush Kush?" I ask the apparent dust bunny in my palm.

"Kushy, cuz. The bud's name's Kushy Kush Kush. Not

Kush Kush. And I'm not Dusty. The name's Chuck Sucka. Got that? Understand?" insists the dust ball. I'm not that stoned. I might be that lonely, but not that stoned— I look to the Mountain of Weed for some logical advice, assistance, a sign of life, something to say back to Dusty— But nothing —The pile of weed is as stoic as can be and these repetitive commercials channeling out of the petty 11-inch TeeVee, are starting to drive me up the wall.

"No, I do not have hemorrhoid flare-ups—I lost my weed— You got a commercial for that?" I swipe my wallet from the table and toss the leather at the screen—Thump, the thing barely slides back—*Side Effects include Diarrhea...*

—lame, find the weed, get high. "Check your chest hair?" Chuck Sucker says. "Don't talk to me if you're going to be rude," I snap back at the lint testicle of spider hair.

He, she, is right though. It is a possibility. I got the lumberjack chest jungle and I've lost my jays down there before. Maybe stumbled into my belly hole— nope, that's just a Jelly Belly, licorice. Not my favorite. "Here," and I hand the wet jelly bean to my good pal Dusty, "Dessert."

I wonder if the old man has got a magnifying glass? Help me in this venture. Maybe a second lamp? What time is it? Six. Fucking dark for six. Dark all day kinda. Old man. Dusty wait here. I put Dusty beside Mt. Greenverest and dart out the room, down the hall, two apartments, knock at Eight O Two. Wait. Listen. Kno...wait. Listen. Might not. I hear something. He's shuffling. I never should have eaten that acid earlier. Stop leaning. Door opened. When?

"I have one. Give me a minute," the Old Man says to me and walks back into his place. From the looks of it, its luxurious compared to mine. Gold. Palace. No, I'm wrong. That's a picture of the Vatican on his wall. What's he got that he wants to give me? And he's back handing me the magnifying glass. The kind you'd use to read a newspaper. How did he know that's what I needed? I thank him. Do that aloud. "Thanks. Very insightful," and I drift away...I have to examine the Duster at the foot of the mound.

*

I got the magnifying glass. Dusty's on the table. Science. Determination. Self-control. Self-reliance. I am here to be myself. "I'm going to strip you apart, one fluffy strand of lint at a time." Tweezers. Clamp. Thread out. Slowly. Ease. This one's called Blonde Sally. The next, Candy Red Rene, Black Beauty Betty, Arabian Knight, Felicity Filament, Fine Wine, one of my pubes, two of the massage therapist's pubes, five eyelashes, sixteen torn resin coated paper doobie tips, and unfolded roaches that I should save. Save I do as I stack the joint bugs beside the mountain.

Lost—

—and—

—found...

...little buggies having a feast upon mini-micro mushrooms that have sprouted in the depths of Dusty's flesh, where it's warm, moist, ideal for fungus, inside the insides of Dusty the Chuck Sucker...and these pin tip sized insects are on my level, deep in the trip. I am the giant disco eye in the sky and it's on, bug rave dust ball, and they got a DJ with eight or more arms, and the magnifier's light flickers and strobes to the rythm of my finger, and the show, dancing praying mantis', stripping caterpillars, dying butterflies, and shit rolling Beatles with scratched records and rainbows to boot. Below, underneath it all, an impenetrable, mummified Bud of Marijuana, Cannabis. The tree's treat. God's gift. Green gratitude. Golden fleeced. Mine. From before. The first, not the last. Not the Bud I dropped tonight, but the OG that got away—

*

That was then. This is now.

*

*

*

*

The doorbell rings. Rings again. The old man wants his

magnifying glass back. Has to read the morning paper come morning. "What time is it?" I ask the bud covered in lint. "5am," it replies. "When did I find you?" I ask. "Earlier," it reminds me. "Like, an hour ago?"

*

Nothing.

        *

                    Quiet.

                            *

Ring. I look at the door. I don't need this thing anymore. Just return it, but the other bud; Where was that one?"

        *

Back on the ground, sifting through the carpet, one hair at a time. Ring. The magnifying glass gets me close, but not close enough. Useless this time. It was a one hit wonder bud...smaller than you. My old friend does not answer. Ring. Knock, knock.

                "Hello?"
                "It's Karen."

"I lost some weed."

"Let me in."

"I can't."

"Do it."

"No."

Ring.

Knock.

Ring.

Knock, Knock.

"Who's there?"

"Karen?"

"Karen who?"

"Stoner."

So,

I open the door.

#04

Brass

Horned

Cannabis

I've always felt the sounds of the club were that of a competing band; glasses filled with rocks & liquor as they clink together, accented by the drops of spillage, the chorus of chatter and laughter, accompanied with billows of tobacco smoke, a public band of patrons within the dancehalls, yet not at odds with the private tunes of brass horns, keys, and drums, from the stage, but a competition neck to neck, entwined in the marathon of the night, run by the vibes of the women on the floor.

Back in my studio apartment, she's a rusty needle on a phonograph caught up with lint accompanied by the public streets, public police sirens, far and wide, overheated by the screeching of bitter wives throwing tongue out their windows at the milkman in the heart of Hells Kitchen, "Turn it down!" — "Turn it off!"— My man coming after you— for leaving me, and she'd whimper and cry, get back up, make her man a meal for after hours, wishing she was fixing a lunch for the milkman instead. Up in Harlem, in this dancehall, this hidden watering hole in the dirt, the bar sounds fulfill the role of the big band's mistress. Here the wives do not pull the strings, our lies and remorse do. The vibe of the women on the floor direct our choices no matter how well the bustle seems as well rehearsed as a studio picture from Hollywood.

"Another round, Sugar?" the black as night African waitress asks my table. With a slight tilt of my derby, and a roll of a silver dollar, I impress her with my Lower Eastside Hebrew smile, and she leans in, whispers in my ear, "You another record producer? We only get your kind when you want something."

"Can't trust a Jew, but I'm here to appreciate you. Disconnected from anything worthy. I'm a card shark from Chicago. I only like black music. Can't sell it."

"Too bad," she turns, takes a step, slow, slow enough to give me time to wrap my arm around this Nubian princess,

Elayah's tail. She's African alright. Family washed ashore in the Caribbean. Enslaved by the Spanish. Moved to America. Fled with her grandparents. Still mails letters back to her parents. Steals the stamps by spending nights with the likes of me.

I've slipped Elayah onto my lap. She saw it coming. Must have a letter to send. SOS, I'm in love with a... I cock the Derby, reveal my eye, my one good eye. Wink. She likes to touch my glass eye. Tink, with her fingertip. Smiles, hugs me. "I missed you," she mumbles into my neck. Wet lips. She kisses my neck, "Missed you so."

Elayah, her eyes are unique enough for a colored girl, green in the club, blue in the morning sun. We've been doing the night covers for quite some time, since July, now we're bearing this Indian Summer, and if you ask me, there's something fishy going down with her lately and I'm not here for the music tonight, I'm here to kill my baby with spite.

Elayah slides off my knee. My chocolate caramel's already gone, off to fix me another drink I suppose, but the fog's too deep to see that far ahead of my future. My glass eye has got the itch. Smoke, the moist-less fog, dries me out. Usually, I carry a case, but my powder's as slim as the humidity in the air. Today I was in a hustle to get uptown. We were down a good $5 on the square. Shlomo had us serving up three-card monte to our Jewish brothers. Trust is tribal, but I was off my game the whole evening. The cards would slip off the box as I spied every colored girl that walked on by. I was bound to spot Elayah out there, making her way to another suitor behind my back— "I need a smoke," I had said to my partner, took a walk to the Park, sparked my ace, tried to forget about the mistress, all for a moment. I ain't married, but no girl I go with have to know I'm single. They know that and then the next thing a fool knows is they start a nesting, and no treasure comes from nesting with a waitress-refugee from the Caribbean, but there ain't no love in losing one either. I was bound to find her tramping around the square. And when I don't, I'll go uptown, catch her at work, catch her on the hook of a swindler with a diamond ring in his pocket.

My honest second half, Shlomo, is not a user of the marijuana. That's why I like him around. I've been in the fog since Chicago. Some Indians brought woven bags full of it to the docks; said they were from Iowa, tried to pull a Christopher Columbus on me, failed. We had them pinned as real Eastern Indians, not Squaws beaten to surrender their land. Gave him two words that I'd keep their cool, play along, say they were Redmen. We made a habit of it, they'd drop off the load, I'd take it to the hooka shop, managed by a Jamaican from the Bronx. Never had I believed the sucker was so easy to con in the Americas. Then again, a Canadian Jew is an anomaly in itself, they thought me as an Italian, Polish-Italian. Suckers, everyone, everyone but the New York Jew. These ball-busters beat me at my own game of 3, then take me for double with a dreidel. That's why I need Shlomo. Sholomo knows his way around a wooden top. Stays dry, stays stone cold, stays within' the law, and says the game is not a game of chance, so not a gamble, and so he's keeping Kosher as he sweeps the cards with me all day long. He won't smoke the pot though. Just six glasses from the vine on Passover. Bless his naive Jewish soul. Get loud kid, forget the man in the cloud.

*

"Empty, amigo?" asks a Latin zoot suit— dark green n' yellow button up, no tie, his chest puffed, neck enamored by an emerald necklace with a pinky ring to match, as his elongated, red finger nail tipped to his bottom lip —He's stepped his green leather shoe on the padded chair beside me. I gotta say, "I don't know you, friend?" with a knife in my pocket, deep in the trench.

"I know your Elayah," he answers, looking into the fog, not me, "That's enough for a drink," and he sits without the final invite, mine. I can kill him now, or I can hear him through. Thought he wanted to sell me a pinch, but it's Caribbean clear where his nose wants to be, "She's a pretty girl," I recognize, secure, braced, and he continues his silent thoughts aloud, "Prettiest thing on the Upper West Side."

Harlem's a far cry from the Upper West Side, but I assume his own heart double-dared to take mine, a double-dare from his one and only so far from reach; the prettiest girl on the Upper West Side.

He pulls a cigarette case, tin,
with a green tint, from his breast
removes a paper tube of refer,
smiles at me,
sets the end on fire,
puff, puff, puff,
the fog thickens, and he takes the first drag,
passing the pain to me. "Use to sell the marijuana Chicago side," I say as I hand the sucker his tube back.

"Cannabis," he corrects me, taking his drag.

"Marijuana, cat," I say, "I know my own."

"You have a problem with cannabis? Even here, you think you not, but you a bigot calling it that," he threatens me, and for no good reason, nothing about our lover's quarrel, not even a spilt bottle of absinth, but over a word, a name, a plant's title.

WHPHEIIT! I whistle my gal back through the dissipating smoke. An arrow, with a magnet, into her ear drum.

Elayah whiffs through the crowd, tray balanced on three of her fingers, twists, and turns and she's back at my table, and setting an hour glass down between the three of us. This new woman was Cuban, tanned over her lighter Spanish skin, and now I see she's been pawned off to me, as Elayah takes her new place in the arms of the zoot suited stranger.

The Latins are both in love, with us. I've certainly lost my cheat on time. My past indulges in the fingernail of the other man, long, dusted, rich. Is this his sister in love with me? She seems in love? Another pair of green eyes shine from the table lamp, and the jewels of the islands. I've known this woman in the past, but I've never laid a kiss on her as of yet. Her name is, "Charo," and she closes her lips, pulls a cigar from her bosom. Hand wrapped, the Thief nods to me, tells me to smell it. Tobacco leaf is fresh, yet the aroma of cannabis is thick. Charo strikes the match, I puff, and I huff, and puff, and huff, and follow me dizzy, the thickness began.

"Dance with me."

"Smooth."

"Have some more."

The Latin pirate cracks a joke.

Difference between a rich man, and a dead man.

A map.

Laughter.

the girls are a fair trade.

Warm.

In the head.

Soften.

The band plays on.

horns. keys. da da drums.

crash

bop bop didie-did he
shaba dapdap did he bop
snap crack smack stack
bap pap pit-tity pit-tity tap

.0

"Please, Benny, dance with her," Elayah pleads with me in the clutches of her solid death of her, this suit in a rumble snuffed silent for this one single night. She bats her eyes, "For me." And with that, I was done, beaten, traded off and spun. Twirled into the bright light, lured by Charo onto the hardwood dance floor...

horns. keys. da da drums.
crash, skittle-te-knock-a-knock-a-knock on wood
bop bop didie-did he-ya
shaba shaba dapdap did he, did he, bop
snap crack-ita-crack-ita smack stack
bapadit-tiy pap-pap pit-tity pit-tity tap, tap, taaap

the brass, the wild woes, the tommy taps of the great band, sung for the Upper West Side, the Harlem Tides, and out of the corner of my eye, I see Pico, her brother, my enemy that is my family, my friend, offer the leader of the bolster of the band, the maestro, the master, offers him a toke from the cannabis cigar— and the lyrics have gone the way of the smoke, echoes, Cannabis, hot; words about the weather, and the fire inside for some sweet grass headed in the heat of the city —and I'm guessing Pico ain't so bad, and clearly Charo is sung by my thunder and my mistress has so easily slipped my mind, therefore, as a gentleman, I take Pico's ear, "Not swag, not leaf, not weed, less marijuana," I moisten my lips, "Cannabis, I fold, rolled in a Cuban, the Cannabis, the Brass Horned Cannabis," and he takes me by the cheeks, first one, then the other, family, and before he can say, "We might all be dead in the same plot," the joint is Keystone Kopped in a hurry. Oval helmet protected coppers tumble in, sets of babbling fools in full swing with pistols and clubs.

And they're pushing and pulling, they're breaking the bottles, setting fire to the bar, arresting coloreds left and right, let the few Jews out, think we're white, unscathed and warned.

But my new girl is a roach, a plague on this city. And her brother, the bottom feeder, picking the hedges from the desperate leftovers of the affluent Upper East Side— Pico and I know we have to get a hold of our girls, get them through the crowd, dodge the deadly screams, and laughter of skulls being popped from a club to a spill on the cracked marbled steps... and get us out the back before the colored boys start to pull their own, tommy guns, ratta tat tat tat, not the drumsticks clacking along the rim, ratta tat tat tat, the tommy guns to defend their waterhole—POP! POP! POP! and I've gotten a hold of Charo, got a lost eye off the Pico and her and instead we're rushed through the crowd of flappers as they tumble out of their high heels, pops droppin' hats, Keystones floppin' tables, crystal champagne sna-a-pop of shattered glass from here to there and literally everywhere. Charo's face speckled, glittered with tiny shards of champagne crystal ice, my throat severed by of solid fin of crystal as I throw Charo through the backstage door— I turn back, see Pico go down in a fury full of lead and the last words from Elayah will forever ring terror through my years, "Run, love," and I was pulled back, out to the street, spun, bled out, but still bleeding. My heart slow, Charo gone, everyone gone, I'm still here, neck bandaged, twenty years late, I'm still on the dock, twisting papers for immigrants, ditching the Nazis, and threading suits of hemp.

#05

ROSEs

ARE

GreeN

When Jack was a puppy it spread the couple's socks along the kitchen linoleum just like the kids do with their toys. Stomp, and kick, crack, and stick, everything, every shape, every robot, and all the paper-clip clamps scattered across the faded kitchen linoleum, snapping their petty metal butterfly wings onto the tips of my toes. Kick his toe against the kitchen fold out; Michael, a father of three, unemployed for over a year, weed-less for a few months short of a year, can't believe how monstrous the little titans have been today. The cat and dog are tough enough. His father never had an indoor dog. Hog stayed indoors. That's what he said of Grandma-ma. This Michael, a stay-at-home dad of three, tried to keep the place clean all day; it was Mom's only request for this momentous day, a day she dwelled on for weeks, the day she didn't really want to come, the day Michael didn't win them the lottery, the day her education was back on hold, the day she had to go back to work, "It's my first day of real work again. Please make the boys pick up after themselves," and then she kissed me, him, us, the family, and vanished for the next ten hours.

1 ½ hours to the city. 15 mins walk from the reasonably priced lot. 1 hr lunch. 15 mins walk back to the lot. 1:15 mins home. Always home 15 mins faster. There is no rhyme, no reason, just an average of 15 minutes and Mom was home, and this was to go on, again, and again—

This was a whole new world for both of them. A world of disciples of life. No one's life, but yours, for now, for years to come. The puppy was house broken by six months. Little son Evan is growing up slow for human years. That's okay. Diapers come with the EBT.

The struggle of Michael's lack of employment due to the heart candy plummeting economy, replaced by candy crush bit coins, and no use for a "presser." Michael was a proud "presser" of the cut machine. The iron blade that cut 100s of heart candies in less than thirty, and he would press it again until he was laid off; whole factory was laid off.

Karen's desire to raise their children on their own without any help from her family took its toll, and they both had felt that if she took the waitressing job, it would do them better than another unemployment check, embellished with another month of EBT. "Boys get in here," Michael called on the three clones of various ages. These flesh-bots, best bots on the market, better than company stocks, rushed in, in a single file line, smallest to largest, into the kitchen, stopping at the doorframe, all looking up at Dad, none let an eye on their mess. Evan was sure to wet himself. Program deficient. No upgrade with EBT. He'll hold it. Ask nicely, "What's going on in here?" Michael asked. Justin, the five-year-old, the eldest model, who stands at 3 feet 1 inch in height, peaks down at the disaster, neck cracks, bolts turn, growing pains, flesh-bots have it worse than their makers, or so the children believe.

"Timmy did it," admits Justin.

"Timmy didn't do this all on his own," speaks authority.

"Johnny too," Justin replied, pushing Johnny, the tiny 3-year old, forward toward the judge.

"What about you?" Michael asks Justin the ring leader.

"Not my toys," he says, and Michael witnesses his eldest son's keen sense of dishonesty, as Michael strings a toy guitar with an, "I belong to Justin," sticker on the body, "What does this say?"

"I don't know how to read," the wise ass little monster of a bean sprout retorts with the poop eating grin he inherited from his grandmother, Karen's mom.

"Go to your room," Michael scolds the child.

"Why?!" Justin screeches as the other two boys snicker.

"Don't laugh at your brother," and now the father is forced to scold them all, wiping his brow, exhausted from the battles of war they had waged in the backyard for hours. Michael thought he was being a fun dad. He had them ding in along the deck, set up water hose machine guns, and stocked his little army full of *Nerf* artillery. The enemy had been two miles out. If General Michael could get his squad organized, then they were sure to hold them off, but Justin, the naturally born traitor had already stockpiled mud-pies behind the shed, and when the war was declared against the camouflaged invisible enemy, Justin ran, ran across enemy lines and immediately began to lob the bombs of mud and muck over the wall, striking the General first, the rest of the army moments after. It was a literal shit show as Michael smelt the vile smell of poop all over his chest. They weren't mud pies, they were wads of doggy droppings and the games were over, Dad needed a shower, the boys needed a shower, the house might need a shower once they track mud, muck, shit, and other rancid debris through the home to reach the barracks. But before all that, these soldiers of chaos need to be hydrated. "Juice or Soda?" the General asked.

"SODA!" hollered the platoon, and with that, the General miraculously pulled a rabbit out of his hat, a carbonated hand-grenade. The boys panted like a litter of pups, and he held the can out before their eyes and shook it, and shook it, and shook it, all before announcing, "Fire in the hole," as he tossed the Coca-Cola Can-Grenade at the brick wall of the home, bursting the compressed carbonation into a mechanical metal ball of spun fury. The soldier puppies ran for cover, in circles, squiggles, tumbles, screams, going for their mud-pies, sending the clumps of wet poop-dirt bombs right at their own leader, the General who had turned on them. These little military pups knew it was now their responsibility to defend their Republic from the, "THE GIANT TRAITOR!"

The Giant takes massive amounts of fire, pelted in every possible place on his body, the steam of fresh doggie do clouding his eye sight. The Giant drops, rolls for cover, an American Ninja soiled in shit, yet still an unstoppable adversary for his own offspring. The General takes hold of the water cannon, sets it on high, aims, there is a PAUSE for effect. The boys freeze. They can sense their doom. Will they be fast enough to avoid it, or will they surrender in fear? Soldier boy Justin turns on his platoon, takes his baby brother as a human shield and informs the Giant Traitor, "We will not be defeated! Drop your weapon, or kill your last born!" but this Father has no intention on losing this battle, "I don't negotiate with children. Meet your fate," and with that he squeezes down on the nozzle releasing a storm of chilled underground H2O directly into the belly of his youngest. Oops. Pops overplayed his hand, overplayed in good fun, but overplayed none-the-less and the baby boy goes down, flat into a pool of mud, and the screams of a 3-year-old stops the war. The middle child is shocked, "You hurt Johnny!" The Giant drops his weapon, guilt, and the frown of a Politician raises his bottom lip and tightens his neck. Justin steps back, wipes his hands clean, instinctually proclaims his innocence, "I didn't do it," while the Giant runs to his littlest soldier's side, lifting him from the mud, wiping the tears from the boy's face, clearing the splatter of mud, ordering any other solider to, "Get him a towel," but Timmy looks to Justin, and Justin just shrugs, "Um, we don't negotiate with Giants?"

"Medic!" Dad yells in an attempt to re-write the game, his guilt of turning on his own platoon turns his own stomach. Justin squats beside his father, playing along with the new narrative, "Sir, yes, Sir!" Michael places Justin's palm onto Johnny's chest, "Take his pulse, medic."

"He's going to live," Medic Justin diagnoses.

"Let's get him in the house, boys. We need to hit the showers before the President returns."

"You mean, Mom?"

"I mean, Mom."

*

Three boys
three deers caught in the headlights of reality

*

"Sir, yes sir!"

The fallen army salutes the reinstated General and run off into
the home, base, barracks. The General remains in the theater
of war. How much trouble are they all going to be in when the
wife sees the yard like this? How much trouble is this General
in? "I gotta clean this up," he says to the ditches, picking up a
shovel, spreading the soil back into the mud lakes, then
remembers, "The boys!" and rushes inside to tend to his
tumultuous army of crazed children he had left to their own
accord.

*

Upon entering his home, Michael finds only the silence from
nothing, but what sounds like the running of a bath upstairs.
The floor is covered in mud. Handprints on the walls, the
refrigerator door, left open, mud on the remaining apples,
mud on the juice boxes, dead juice boxes on the kitchen table,
and this man is in a heap of hell by nightfall.

*

The bathroom door is still open, piles of muddy poop clothes
on the floor, steam rising from the bath, the hot nozzle has
been turned on, but the place is absent of soldiers. Where are
the boys? "Boys!" Michael yells, no longer playing the role. He
turns off the hot water, ramps up the cold, then heads out to
fetch the naked beasts hiding in their shared room.

*

Each kid has taken shelter on their bed, under their covers.

Dad stands in the doorframe, "No one's in trouble, just get washed up." One by one little heads uncover themselves. "We're not?" asks the eldest. "Not today," says the Michael. "We don't believe you," worries Timmy. "Don't worry," the Dad knows it's all his fault.

"We don't believe you," Justin the leader admits.
"Bath, now," the Dad.
"You first," negotiates Justin.

Michael looks at himself in the mirror, he is covered in disgust. He looks behind himself. He, the General himself, has tracked twice as much mud into their home as the three boys were even capable of, and the boys laugh, and Michael laughs, and that laughter turns into screams of getting clean and clean and clean and cleaner still.

*

With fifteen to twenty minutes before the President's caravan arrives home, Michael hits the TV, afternoon cartoons, gathers the children, and passes out for a little shut eye before he must report to the boss.

*

The garage door opens, closes, and Michael awakens at the sound of the entrance door as it unlatches and shuts closed. She is home. The house is clean, his work is done, and supper warms in the oven. "Hey babe, how was the first day?" his wife asks Michael as he turns the corner. His first day of *Daddy Day Care*? Perfect.
"How was your day?" he asks as opposed to answering.
"I brought you something," she says, "For being such a supportive husband." And from behind her back, Karen, Michael's beautiful, loving wife, presents him with a quarter bouquet of flowers— Cannabis flowers, purple, green, highly glittered marijuana flowers, buds in a bouquet, covered in highly potent kief. "Let's put the boys to bed and roll one," she says kissing her good husband. "You brought me flowers."

06

THE UNTOLD STORY of
WENDY
the WEED
of the
WEST

Many a great heroes have been memorialized, immortalized, and extended lies throughout all the American histories—heroes like Paul Bunyan, Pecos Bill, the Dude, John Henry, Yosemite Sam, Betsy Johnson, Jimi Hendrix, Mister Kincaid, and even Ronald McDonald Reagan and his endless jar of jelly beans. But America, like all great countries, 'cept we're the greatest even when we suck, is also known for a few too many conspiracies and whatnots. Well, in fact, this here story about Wendy the Weed of the West, is assumed to be as conspiratorial as it may sound to the staunchest conservative, but trust me twice, and disbelieve the loudspeaker from the youtube and remember this—

—this be one of the truest tall tales of them all.

PROLOGUE: A few yearly moons before the Gold Rush, flat dab in the middle of the Civil War, California was still a quaint state, with only a few stragglin' settlers who had found their way into the overgrown Redwood Forests that stuffed the North West. Said to be an easier life up there, said to be...quaint.

*

One couple by the names of William and Wynona had found themselves a secluded patch of land surrounded by the giant trees along a fresh water stream, only a few miles inland from the shore. They had plenty of fish and soil for a small vegetable garden and dinners. William, a fine craftsman by trade, built them a cabin straight from sixteen surrounding Redwoods, leaving tall stumps to be used as the home's foundation and frame. It has been said, this Redwood home stood four stories tall, for one good real reason alone—

In order for Wynona to grow her Cannabis patch
closer to the sun.

See, Mr. William had been raised on a Hemp farm in East Virginia. Back then in them times, the small colony turned state still had good relations with the Queen of England, and the export of the plant was still mighty profitable. But young William took a liking to construction rather than the farming life and this was sort of a disappointment to his folks.

Well, William figured, to make his Mama happy, it be best to marry a wife from a nearby farm. He had always taken a liking to Miss Wynona since they were tots, and then again during the high school times, even though there weren't no high schools back then, only schools of life and parts of that were for getting high. Wynona was the Jessabelle that introduced him to her own hobby of growing the female version of the Hemp stalks— the Cannabis flowers.

Soon, once William was allowed at the age of twenty-one, he

put that golden ring on Ms. Wynona's finger and had themselves a preacher from the outskirts do the wedding, and that was fine for Wynona's Mama, but her Pops wasn't so thrilled, but he was stewing about other situations regarding his daughter. Ms. Wynona had gone and corrupted the family's fine fields of male, fabric weaving Hemp with her toxic flowers.

See, ever since she started growing them stinking flowers, the cannabis, the workers would much rather make music and the arts, 'stead of tending to Pa's money-sprouting stalks of miracle making stuff.

Pops had to let young William marry his daughter, he needed a pansy, a stooge of love to do whatever necessary to be with his daughter. "Sir Wynona, sir. Might I have your daughter's hand in marriage, sir. I promise to love and to keep her, to death do us part, and..."

"You promise to move her as far away from my crops as possible?" was all Pops cared about.

***   ***

The Honeymoon was far in the West. It was a midnight trek from here to nowhere short of the sea. William knew what needed to be done and packed himself and the little lady up and set out to travel on out to the wild, wild West.

***   ***

Saddened and anxious without her flowers, Wynona and William found themselves knocking on Indian doors to tame the pain along the lonely, grassy plains. The Native folks would tell this struggling couple stories of a place where the cannabis flowers grew plumper, and that place was out West exactly where they were headed, close to the sea. Empty handed, and months away from settling down, Wynona traded these Indians a few of her homegrown Virginia seeds for a bag of cannabis cigarettes to assure an enjoyable jaunt of a Honeymoon to home. And these Cannabis cigarettes gave them visions from the Future, instructing them to cross South of the Rockies instead of the North. The couple had been visited and led to the South by the not yet notorious Donner Party, ghosts of the future, who would tell their tale of death and cannibalism as they led William and Wynona safely South of the Rockies, then up the Coast to the Redwood Forests, and just vanish straight into nothing, probably off to the tragic future; but not as far North as Oregon as predicted.

*

Wynona spent the first few summer months growing her garden directly on the fertile ground of the Redwood Forest. By early autumn, William had finished construction of their giant home. Wynona immediately took advantage of the rooftop that was only towered by a few more feet of Redwood tops.

The sun couldn't get through the trees, the roof would be much more suitable for a garden. Wynona and William raised the soil up with a pulley system and meticulously spread the dirt along the sunken rooftop that allowed for a good six feet worth of fine Redwood soil. At first, they used the same pulley to water the roof earth, but soon enough, William had the plumbing system up and running until the autumn fog began creeping in from the nearby ocean helping keep the seedlings moist in the morning and then throughout the night. The fog became Wynona's favorite natural phenomenon as she made her way up every day to bathe in the mist as it consumed her and her darlings atop the home her husband built.

These conditions were spot on for the plants. They grew at a rapid rate and Wynona could have never imagined how bountiful the Cannabis plant could be in the West. The Native's stories were true, and for this she was ever so grateful. In return for what dreams may come, Wynona and William would sing to their plants in the morning, again in the afternoon, then tell them *Tall Tales* at night, with the faith that a tall tale would make their darlings even taller, and that they did, if anything in this story is true, be sure it be those plants were ginormous.

The medicinally magical weeds seemed to want to outdo their rivals the Redwoods, and though some may say that is nearly impossible, the bushes atop the couple's home were an exact four hundred and twenty times the size they grew back in the fields of East Virginia. Exact cubic.

Then the couple done died.

No one knows exactly when, but they both croaked at the very same second, with the very same fate. Both were crushed under the collapsed roof of their very own home. Been speculated that Wynona was singing them plants a song at the time, while William fluffed their green feathers; then they heard a crack, could have even been the rumbling sound of the start of some crushing, but before either of them knew nothing, the whole house collapsed by the mighty weight of the Cannabis farm on their rooftop.

Now, now, don't get discouraged that this story ends here 'cause in America, tragedy tends to lead to good fortune and vice versa, and every which way 'cept hell; choices, options, America. Anyhow—

Shortly after our lovely departed pioneers of Redwood Tip Top Cannabis agriculture, were squashed from limb to limb and buried below the tree planks of the home, the soil from the roof, and the massive medicinal Cannabis flora, a bona fide Marijuana Miracle occurred. Since the house was built completely out of Redwood and such, it naturally decomposed right there, and real quick. Guessin' the forest really needed to do some clean up.

Now, since all that Cannabis fell down as well, the local forest critters came around in hordes getting their edibles and such. These banquets of Cannabis culinary collectives gave way to seed dispersal. That's a scientific term for animals eating stuff and spitting out the seeds, like we people do with an orange. So, these here critters spit out all the Cannabis seeds right there into the pile of debris that used to be the house of William and Wynona, bless their souls.

Few days then passed after all the seed spittin' and those little unborn baby plants sprouted seedlings and absorbed their spiritually endowed nutrients from Wynona's deceased parts. A new forest done started to sprout in the middle of them Redwoods, and that there forest was made up of monstrously large and incredibly potent Cannabis plants— a suitable legacy for the fallen couple.

***   ***

William?

Well nobody really knows 'bout his remains. Just became dirt I reckon. All peoples discuss is Wynona's bones. Kinda not fair if you think on it...

but then again,
he built the house that fell done down
and killed them both
together
with the weed

***   ***

Like I already told ya, nobody really went up state all that much, which gave this new plantation free-reign to grow in great abundance, void of any worries or concerns. These Cannabis plants spread out all along them Redwoods. They didn't need the higher levels of sun no more 'cause Wynona's soul was makin' them stronger, and more resilient than ever. Them plants had adapted to this new way of being. Within a few short months, this plot of land, which stretched out nearly to the shore, was once known for its vibrant red bark, but now shined another color, an emerald glow. The plants spread themselves into the shape of a loosely shaped triangle, and they were happy.

As with all good things, trouble's just down wind and around 1848 there came this new surge toward the West, and an even greater urge to build homes, and to build them Red. The lumberjacks started filing into the North West, first two at a time, then families, then those loner lumberjacks married the daughters and had more sons, and the sons had even more daughters, and they started building towns, and those towns took up space, and the Cannabis forest caught wind of this, 'cause suddenly there were less trees around, so the breezes broke through with much greater ease. These winds of change were so strong that they would blow the sticky golden kief right off the plant's leaves and flowers. The Cannabis figured maybe they'd be found. If they were found, then maybe the men would get high. If the men got stoned then maybe the women would bake them into cookies and treats. And if the women got baked, then their sons and daughters would be sure to follow suit and everyone would stop cutting down trees and start growing more weed, but this didn't happen, no sir. Instead, the men did find them weeds, but these men didn't know much of this strange growth all along the land where their precious houses would be. In the East they had heard of the medicinal properties of these plants, they might have even known of the recreational use, but the newspapers back East were filled with misinformation. The bottles of weed juice were labeled as poison, and even though a Doctor was able to give a prescription for such, he only did so with a warning that you might not be able to feel your face, you could even lose your legs, and you're sure to have nightmarish visions like the Indians, and nobody back then wanted to be a like an Indian, but they sure did want those Redwood houses.

See, back in those times, only the Natives knew of the truly unique aspects of the Cannabis. The white man, well, he didn't know Cannabis from Apples, and Johnny Appleseed was a star, a hero to the American man, a hero we celebrate with apple pie day to day, but not the Marijuana. What they didn't realize is that the Cannabis can talk. The Cannabis could even take a walk if it felt threatened, and that's just what happened in the Emerald Triangle. Mama plant was as large as a plant could ever grow, 'bout 50 feet in diameter at 25 feet tall. The Papa plant, that kept her fertilized, was half her size and had grown most of himself around her, almost like he was protecting his lady. It was a most suitable system to spread themselves with ease. Mama would catch the wind, shaking her stems and flowers, releasing her seeds. The seeds would fall upon Papa's enormous hemp leaves and bounce right off to great lengths— new soil.

Now, Mama Cannabis, well, she was completely infused with the soul of Wynona, as Papa had been infused with William's I guess— See, that's where he came on in — Been said that being sprout right from Wynona's own belly was like the plant was Wynona's daughter, and when them Lumberjacks had started chopping into her children, there was nothing much a plant could do to defend its self. Papa Plant swore to hold the fort and set Mama free to find a new place to plant her legs. Mama, with no other plan in sight, uprooted herself and walked her way out of the forest, south side, avoiding the Lumberjacks and their wives. She had to steal clothes to cover herself, took to learning how to ride a horse from a blind stableman, found a gambler who showed her how to play a mean game of cards and named her Wendy.

Well, Wendy the Weed of the West, made her way along the American landscape as an Outlaw, possibly the most notorious woman Outlaw never spoken about in these here Tall Tales of the great states. That's what Mama Cannabis had become— an Outlaw of the state, an Outlaw of the people, yet a friend to the natives, a lover of the fresh water rivers, all-the-while dropping seeds all along her trails wherever she did go, letting her new babies grow despite the coming storm of adversity.

***   ***

My Grand-Daddy came across Wendy the Weed just east of the Rockies, in the new state of Nevada, early 1860's. There weren't nothing there back then, 'cept an Outlaw population, lots of dust, and a few freewheeling gamblers. This desert of a state was a place where a criminal could get a bottle of whiskey, take three whores, shoot six men, and call it a night in the local streets of dirt without even a thought of a jail cell or a quick ride on the gallows. It had been a warm Nevada night and my Grand-Daddy, a simple cowhand, and the boys had brought the game of black jack out onto the road 'stead of keeping their game inside the heated bar. Mellon, the barkeep, preferred you called it a saloon, "But five bottles of JD, some watered-down brandy, some poison worse than moonshine, and two homely dancing girls too sweaty to dance is a far cry from any sort of saloon I ever been too," said the dark figure half way down the road, in a cowboy hat, holding the reigns of its horse. In unison, the whole damn table of card players, killers, and politicians, rose to attention. "That's mighty loud for a stranger just settling into town, son," said the fat Mayor of this makeshift street.

Now, this wasn't your average game of 21 these boys were playing; the stakes were steps higher than a few coins. This was "The 21." Twenty-one men invited, twenty-one crooked cowboys playing for key roles in this here's new state government. Now this Mayor had won enough hands so far to reach such a peak, knocking down his competitors to senators, school administrators, land dumpers, deputies, and regulators, that he was sure going to hold this title of Govna for the rest of the hands, yet like any old game of Black Jack or any old card game there is, there's always a dumb-luck chance another hand'll come around and cut into your pot. But this evening, it was the Pot herself standing at the side of the table, taking a seat of her own— Wendy the Weed of the West — And she was already fuming, and the fumes were fun.

At first sight, Wendy looked just like any G-d fearing Outlaw on the desert floor toting her tired stallion. But now that Wendy had taken the seat away from my Grand-Daddy, who had lost too many hands to ever be more than a dust sweeper anyhow, her massive green leafed clothing and red hair became more prevalent, and it was obvious she wasn't no man, maybe a woman, but not the kind of woman they had ever seen before. This lady was green and intoxicating.

"You some sort of Indian giver? You wanna bet your hide on a piece of land?" the Mayor of No Town challenged Wendy.

"That's right," Wendy done said, "And me and my babies want it by a river." Wendy removed her hat and showed her betting chips, a bowl full of prime Cannabis seeds. Seeds none of them had ever seen before.

"We ain't betting for gold, or them farmer's food," said the Mayor, "We're playing for higher jobs and lower landscapes.

So, if you're willing to be a cow hand to any one of these here men, then keep that seat, and I'll dish you a hand."

With a tip of her worn and torn cowboy rim, Wendy just said, "If it's higher stakes that you want, then might someone have a little fire to get me started?" Six boys were quick to light her a match, and a few wasted a little butane all to reach over the table to light her smoke, but one got to her from the side as he whispered spit into her pretty green ear, "I know of your Cannabis kind. You ain't gonna fool me one bit. Smoke yourself blind, and I'll be taking your pot one leaf at a time." Wendy smirked. A poet he was not, and she just exhaled right into the man's choppers, and that cowboy's eyes went red, his mouth went cotton, and the Mayor, the table's Dealer, threw a single card to each and every one of the 21 players while Grand-Dad dusted the road around them with a make-shift broom as the table played through their numbers.

Wendy the Weed of the West reclined in her chair, sucked herself down, and the fumes from her own ever so potent leafy-self had everyone seeing double aces, purple jacks with crescent queens, tens that looked like dimes, and drifting scenes of Native visions about wolves, eagles, dancing girls, and desert worms in their boots.

> The boys kept calling for another, and another, "Hit me. Hit me. Hit me again. Again. AGAIN!" - BUST - "Darn it" - And again - "Hit me. Hit me. Okay, hit me," - BUST - "Darn gone it!"

This kept going around busting each and every one of them cowboys 'till Wendy and the Mayor played alone as the last two gamblers in the new Nevada state. Mayor, "but you can call me Govna little lady."

"You ain't won yet civilian," said the wind from Wendy's lips. The game had done the dealt, and now they were eye to eye, smoked to toked, hope to croak, and Wendy simply said, "You might be ready to send me two or three of them Jacks or Jokers, but know me well, and know me pure— I'm a One Hit Wonder weed, so I got me an Ace, and I'd like just One Hit in return." The Mayor didn't hesitate, no use in biding time now, so he tossed her a card, and that card was a King and Wendy cracked her neck stem and grinned, "21," and Grand-Daddy dropped the broom and the dust ball blew out and things became highly unclear, and a little bit foggy.

***   ***

If this had been a regular card fight that would be the end of it—Twenty Men folded, gone bust, with a woman walking away with her earnings—But when you're throwing down cards for government power jobs, fences, borders, wells, rivers, and laws, well that's when the guns come out when a woman wins the world. But this wasn't any old girl. Wendy was more a stranger than your average wandering weed so these boys came out guns a blazing not just aimin' and shot up poor Wendy like a dead horse hanging tail side from a tree for target practice.

***   ***

After them Outlaw lawmakers unloaded all them pistols into poor Wendy's gut there was an eerie silence in the night air. It was a strange new calm for all them boys. From gambler to gambler their senses began to change. All them peepers went as red as an Arizona stone, scratched up with streams of blood and blue all across the whites of their eyes. Their yapping mouths had stopped chattering 'cause all they could do was smack them dusty lips together again and again, seeking some sort of saliva, their mouth spit that had nearly all dried up along their wooden teeth; felt like cotton in their mouths. A few of the busted gamblers tried to stop their own laughter until succumbing to the toasty smoke in the air and plain old busted out into some absolute comedic madness that shook up the entire table.

Grand-Daddy, well, he just stared straight at Wendy, smoke rising from various bullet points of entry on her leafy figure, and smiled and shot her a little wink, proud to see them woman kind hold herself together as such. See them bullets shot right through Wendy the Weed, scorching her leaves and flowers, then soaring to some aimless end in the desert. Now, Wendy the Weed was fuming ready to keep the game going as her smoking poison toasted the entire table. She playfully addressed the Mayor with an ultimatum for setting fire to something he knew nothing about, "I'll play 'till you can't see, or 'till ya'll fall a slumber from my lumber." The Mayor looked to his other boys, but they were too stoned to know nothing by now and Wendy just laid out the rules, "We'll play 'till the sun, but once yer done, sleeping sound, forgetting you smoked more than a pound, then I've won. I'll plant myself by the river and I expect no tourists. You'll protect me, you'll harvest me pure, and you'll ship me to every single shore. Them be the new stakes to play."

"Deal," said the Mayor, "But the boys play back in, too," expecting to win, and slid the deck of cards to the Weed, and she shuffled, and blew.

Most of them boys were too mellow to really want to play and one had even called it quits snoring on the floor so Grand-Daddy took up his seat. Wendy flipped them cards left and right, rainbowed them a good twenty-one times, which sent all them cowboys into a sort of Cannabis trance. Then she'd cut up the deck and send the fat man his first card, a number 2, then herself an Ace, and then that Mayor got himself a broken-hearted Queen, which was 22, and that's a bust. Bust, Bust, Bust, Hit Me, Hit Me, One More, 23 - BUST AGAIN! And Wendy dealt herself an Ace to join her Jack, 21! And this sort of luck just kept coming to Ms. Wendy the Weed of the West.

Wendy had demoted Senators into wranglers, wranglers down to chicken farmers, farmers became well watchers, and the mayor, still losing, kinda figured his cheating ways of reading cards and stabbing knives in the backs of gamblers was going to promote him straight up to governor king of the land by the time the sun rose. The fat man was wrong about that. As the night kept crawlin' by, the Mayor began a worry some sort of train of thought, an intense paranoia, the anxiety of a lost world, intensified by his lack of knowledge about this smoke coming from Wendy the Weed of the West. The fat man's eyelids started to tremble as he tried to keep them open, loosing count of the cards, and thought if he cleaned three more bottles of bourbon he could drink away the pain even though she had warned him, "You can only smoke the pain away. If you keep up that a drinking, you're surely gonna rot your liver and make the brain a little bit more the lame." But the Mayor didn't hear her, nor did he follow her words.

By the time the sky started to change from a solid black with speckled stars to a popping purple, the entire table was sound asleep, stoned on the dirt floor, and the Mayor, well, the Mayor had grown pretty sick and knew he had been beat. What's a fat man from the South to do surrounded by sleeping Outlaws and woman taking him down? That's all he could think under the influence of the drink. That's puzzling confusion he's gotta figure out before he hits the deck one more time, tumbling like loose grass down from a leader to a loser. This fat man was raised white in a white man's theater of a Civil War, with power in his palms, and insults dribbling from his nose. Ten hours sooner or so, this Mayor of new town at the table saw himself ruling this new Nevada with an Iron Hand like his Papa's pals in Texas. He planned to mine the whole state, have the Orientals lay track like a crossword puzzle, fool them blacks to think they got real rights, trick the natives to field the sand 'stead of the rivers, and sell the ladies to the presidents and congressmen alike. He had dreams of owning all the gambling games, and hanging men left and right to show his power and his precious might. But now he's stoned, and drinking. His mind's loud with guilt for such reckless ideas and mayhem. The wind of the rising sun has spun Wendy's wafting fumes into a table top tornado with the Mayor trapped in a sand storm of exhaustion, regret, and wonder. Now Ms. Wendy the Weed, almost completely charred, burnt nearly to a complete crisp, had one last thing to ask of this fat, post-rich, country boy of a politician, "When you look to the sky this early, stoned as you could be, drunker than a town house full of whiskey, and poorer than a rabbit with no bunnies to play, what color you think your heart ought to be?"

The Mayor rubbed his eyes, flipped the last card he'd been dealt, and found himself a laughing Joker prancing along on the red, white, and black card. He looked straight into the red lined eyes of the Weed, then up to the sky illuminated by the coming sun. His heart fell low, his soul was deep down in his toes, and all the Mayor could find on his tongue was the one word that gave him a better know how of what was deep in his heart, deeper in his soul, and spread out all over the sand, and he sung out "the Blues."

Wendy stood herself right up with a tip of her hat. She had won all the games at play, and had a few words left to spin, "Now boys and the fat man, you've seen things you ain't never gonna explain. And I'm sorry to say you ain't never gonna feel this high again, no matter how hard you try. No matter what seeds you sow, or what weeds you grow, you won't have a night like this to try and win again. As I've come to see it, lucky men only get one option to smoke their sorrows away. You're just too lucky to come across a day like today for a second time. Now I'll leave you this desert, for it don't grow nothing good, and you and these Outlaws can run this state, and you'll run it all away, but just know you won't never forget my name. See, I'm the only Weed of the West, and I'm the most potent green skinned lady you'll ever come by. You can chop me down. You can burn me sweet. You can ruin the soils so I won't grow, or turn off the lights so I can't breathe. But one thing you ain't never gonna know, is my seeds are stronger than your toughest bow. So, I'm gonna stroll, slow, and tame to the river that I won, to the river where I'll set my seeds to sow. Now sit right back, Mr. Mayor, and have another toke, because see here fat man, you're the butt of my here..." and that's where the Mayor interrupted her, sold by her story, sold by her fire, standing right up, nearly buckling at the knee, but with a shotgun in his hand and said, "No, you're the butt of my here joke," and shot that now dark skinned crispy stick of a thing into ash n' pieces, sending poor Wendy's hat full of children to the sky.

Grand-Daddy tried his best to collect the ash and take it back to where she might had come from, leaving the Mayor to think that he had been done with these weeds and seeds, and things. Sure, if the Mayor had known his place and just let his hand fold he might have been a friend to the green ones, but he missed his very own jackpot, and that shotgun did a better job at seed dispersal than the critters of the Emerald Triangle and the seeds had soared to the heavens and back, falling all along the American landscape growing from coast to coast.

***   ***

So next time you're swinging and singing about the ganja that grows whenever and wherever they be, and you're wondering just how that all came to be, well just look up to the heavens and remember the story of Wendy the Weed of the West, the one tall tale that's been repressed, and never take the plant for granted, never try to outsmart her, 'cause as you know by now, the Cannabis is always gonna win every day in, one card at a time, state to state to put them in line. No matter what you call her, no matter what you fear, never call her a crime, for it's the fool who'll burn time.

#07
CHRONiCALLY
iNSANE
w/PAiN

The door would have broken his knuckles. He wouldn't want to do that. He needed a shock to the nerves, a cut, just enough to replace the constant pain in his bones. Not the door. Instead he'd punch a hole through the drywall. If he's lucky he'd hit a stud and just break a knuckle or two. That would do the trick, man. That would take his mind off it for a minute or two, all the clinical Chronic Pain. Then he'd write his wife a letter, maybe a poem. Take the time to fill out a job application, or possibly pay a bill. The throbbing pain of a couple broken fingers would allow him to grip a pencil in his good hand again. The tightened carpel tunnel couldn't compete with the intentionally inflicted wounds. A moment. It would be brief, but he had a moment to use his other hand again. He could write something 'till he grimaced from the shock of tendons brushing against the fleshy tunnel in his wrist. He should smoke some weed now. The weed will prolong the moment. Distract him from the pains. Distract him from the insane.

I got all sorts of pain man.
I got it in my soles.
I got it in my head,
I got it in my elbows.

I'm about to see red.

I got woman leaving home blues,
I got money troubles too.
I got nothing so good,
Not even a clue.

Muscles burn down through my spine,
My head rocks with sorrows, The shoulders ain't kind.

I want to kick away tomorrow.
I want to save a today.
I play the victim, and say it's okay.

There's nothing I want so much as to do,
Nothing I to think.
When the pain is bursting,
I throw down and sink.

Liquor hits the spot,
Then I fall down and cry.
While whisky burns my throat,
I puke 'til I die.

Beer doesn't make it better,
Sweet drinks are a lie.
Sour spritzers in bed,

I'm still about to see red.

Took pain pills for migraines,
Popped Valium all day.
At first, I felt funny,
Then a train wreck in May.

I could never wait tables,
Can't bus like bum.
My legs would all buckle,
My hands can't get me to cum.

Telemarketing the phones,
But the hips couldn't sit.
And you know what that means?
Yup, I just had to quit.

Moved down to the first floor,
Instead of the sixth.
Still carry groceries,
Some things you can't fix.

I wept in the showers,
To fend off the stress.
Spent months watching TV,
Oh fuck, what a mess.

Starts to burn from relaxing,
So, I walked seven miles.
Get home, and just slept,
Cause awake I can't smile.

When I open my eyes,
There's a stir in my bones.
The flesh all around them,
Just needs to get stoned.

Lost sight of my life,
Can't find the time.
Tried to rewrite a story,
Where my world knows no glory.

Now I smoke and I toke,
as much pain stain away.
I take dabs off my finger and that's okay.

I roll doobies of gold,

I eat browns by the dozen.
There is safety in numbers or so I am told.

I'm a career pothead to calm the strain,
The only thing to fight this corruption,
This obsession of pain.

See the weed lifts the lows,
The CBD fills my soul,

The one thing is this Cannabis plant,
it just friggin' knows.

If you think that's bad,
Well fella,
You've never gone mad.

The Doctors tried pills,
They even tried some tests.
Yet the weed fills my brain,
'Cause Cannabis is the best.

He sets the pencil down. Things don't have to be as bad as they seem, once they don't seem so bad. That's the point of view he claims as his nerves sting less. The weed assists his mind in distraction. Distraction can be with a clear thought, through inspiration, what nots. Things seem brighter. He took another sip from his vape, and a dab on his lip. Two of them will clear the air, two of them will dent in the walls, and two of them will give him...

...a moment.

#08

MINISTeR

MIs

tER

A copious number of adult aged children piled into the outdoor venue by the hundreds to hear him speak. Twenty gigantic amplifiers had been set up along the open field of golden and crisp grass, grass that has turned to dust from the drought in the dry heart of the city. This was not the crowds of tomorrow, these were the crowds of right now, and yester-year. Mick Jagger and his Rolling Stones' recordings blasted from the speakers— Sympathy for the Devil, Miss You, Can't You Hear Me Knocking, speckled with other tunes like The Who's Amazing Journey, Journey's Wheel in the Sky, Norman Greenbaum's Spirit in the Sky, AC/DC's Who Made Who, and the standard of Jimi's Purple Haze.

These tunes were carrots covered in caramel for the masses. Psychedelic Pop posters that lined the city's thin wooden boards surrounding construction sites promised a day off from the grind, a way to get to *reality*, a door opening to their perceptions. Was it a flashback to the sixties for the youth of today, or was it just a Minister out of touch with tomorrow?

*

The masses were taken by surprise when their medley of drugs had been confiscated at the park's entrance in a bizarre exchange. Security guards, clothed in modern knight armor barring machetes and Uzis stood stoic at the gates, as men in black ski-masks patted down the audience's pants, one by one, reaching into their pockets, unzipping their purses, stealing, and trading the crowds unlabeled zip lock bags, bottles of pills, vape pens, and acid tabs for a strange substitution— bags of weed for money, acid for blank checks, gift cards, bitcoin, and pennies with dimes for quarters of hash.

*

The baffled crowd impatiently waited for Minister Iah to take his place behind the podium. They weren't so much impatient to hear this man speak, it was their purpose for coming in the first place, they were impatient to get back their drugs and booze. They were all jonesing for a fix which turned into a human smorgasbord of itches, and ruckus, spit fights and titty-twisters, melvins and charley horses, beat downs and rape. It was but a general hysteria, just about anyone would have expected from a society stripped of their goods despite the fact that all of them were now a little richer in the pocketbook.

*

The morning hours passed without a sign of the Minister. Out of pure exhaustion and sudden boredom the crowd had begun to sit on the dusty grass. Their legs were exhausted, the sun was hot, the sky was muggy, and the loss of goods had turned from annoyance, to anger, to need. "I just need something to help me deal with this," was a common topic of discussion amongst the audience of now thousands.

The psychedelic sixties were over, replaced with smooth jazz. This was nearing a breaking point for anyone with a pair of ears stuck wondering why they bothered to attend the speech of a Minister who promised them a psychedelic future on a poster.

Their stomachs ached from hunger, their bodies weakened from dehydration, their migraines...unfortunately beginning to appreciate the irreplaceable Kenny G? They were all still unsure why they were all so suddenly very rich in their pockets.

"The bouncer gave me six hundred bucks for the one joint I had," a girlfriend says to her boy. He leans in for a kiss. She's too ill to be romantic, "I'm not in the mood."

"Neither am I," he admits.

*

Minister Iah, dressed in black and white, has taken to the podium to speak to the tired, the sick, and now that he's stripped them of their intoxicants, the spiritually poor. No one had noticed he took the stand. No one had risen, no one had applauded. The Minister is just too far to be seen. The Minister might have been on Mars if it wasn't for his microphone, and the desperate ears of an audience who had sacrificed their weekend for a better tomorrow. Isn't that what they have done? Too late now, no one could even think for themselves after baking in the hot sun without nourishment, water, and drugs.

*

And he began to speak.

*

"I have made a trade with you to hear me clearly. I have lined your pockets with gold. Fast cash in exchange for your poison, and now, wrought with the realities of a hoax, how do you feel?"

The crowd, too ill to respond,
conforms to listen with their blind eyes.

"Equally as pitiful? Or now more eager to learn?"

The crowd doesn't understand. Why is he doing this? They must know more. Listen, for once. Don't hear, don't watch, listen. What else is there to do, they have no stimulation. Some begin to stand. Why stand, but to see as well? Those who do stand, stand with the assistance of each other. Their neighbor is their cane, your neighbor is your crutch; we are their bearings. "Lean on me, when you're too weak to lean into them," the Minister rewrites the old adage.

*

"For those who are hungry, I assume you are always hungry. For those who are starved, I assume you are starved from abandoning the salvation of your spiritual dimensions, lost amongst the maze of fire and brimstone that you cannot see, for the smoke billows, clouds, looks like heaven, smells like H-E-Double Hockey Sticks."

*

An Elderly lady has fallen. A new born has been crushed.
The Fat Man is poorer still.

*

"Haven't you traded enough of your purpose for the petty mortal accomplishment of trying— Trying to get higher, more known, celebrated by every pulse tapping on our web of artificial intelligence?"

*

Scattered through the crowd, a few have snuck carob and

toast in their socks. These few have begun to applaud. They are a sorry lot if ever there has been one. Selfish, indulgent, keeping their drugs for this very moment so they themselves may lead the choir in a chorus of none-sensical sheepishness.

*

Outside the park, curled around its circumference are lines of people still panting to get inside, past the gates, into the inner circle they have been fooled into paying for, but the scrutiny of the security guards has been distracted by a Tall Fat Man clothed in the finest of suit-leather, adorned with diamond cufflinks, barefoot, and topped with a weathered derby. This Tall Fat Man negotiates with the Command; he's bartering, something for something they already have, for something they have stockpiled for the Minister; the people's goods.

*

"This hunger will buckle your knees at the sight of your friends too weak to stand on their own. Your stomachs will turn from the pain of your bodily existence that cowers at the thought that you have no control of your own fate. That your destiny is no more sensible than your mortality."

*

The Minister stops to sip from his crisp glass of ice water. His thin, fleshless lips, pitter-patter smoochy-smooch into the mic blasting the slippery, sloppery, slurp-a-loo pattern, of an elderly man wetting his lips upon a crystal crevasse... and then he continues...

*

"You demand aspirin, ibuprofen, opiates for the masses— the massive headache you endure from doing business with others. You ask the bartender for a drink, dry, or on the rocks? Maybe you need a smoke; tobacco or marijuana? Sex on the Beach, or California Kush? Some turn towards relations— Sex in numbers, clean, careful, planned, protected, killers, all of you. Others stretch their absence of spirit with pay-per-view Yogis and think you'll all be but forgotten, but soon enough...

—the sickness returns."

*

The head of security approaches the Tall Fat Man. The Fat Man lifts the guard's facemask and questions this authority, "What is so important that you are holding up the line?"

"To the back of the line."

"Are you sure there is a line to be a part of?"

"To the back of the line."

"Are you content with your menial form of authority?

"To the back of the line."

"Are you happy, snappy, crappy, and dull?"

*

"Never turn your eye from your faults, for your faults define your time. Your faults are the candy canes your Lord and Savor eats away from your souls. The Devil is already here, buried under your landfills, boiling your priceless chocolates until they melt. The Savior, my Leader, your King, is upon the highest peak waiting to cure you of the disease."

*

"Nonsense," says the Tall Fat Man.

*

"I only speak the truth in puzzles, but puzzling is the truth."

The crowd understands this Minister.
They know how, why, and where they are to go.
They came with a mission and that mission is confused.

"Everyone likes to be told I have an answer
and answer you all I will to him.
So, listen as I lie, my head upon your hearts."

And the Tall Fat Man knows the Minister is no different than
the unlucky horse clamped down with weighted shoes.

*

The Tall Fat Man tips his derby, drops a single loaf of bread
into his palm and hands it to the commander of security.
"Bread?" the guard asks. "My suit is stuffed with various
kinds of leavened bread," the Tall Fat Man retorts. "Is that
why you're so repulsively heavy?" the guard spikes with an
ungrateful grin. The Tall Fat Man reaches into his pant pocket
and pulls out fat stacks of Benjamins that he hands out to each
and every guard. He becomes a little shorter with every stack
he extinguishes from his account.

*

"You've wandered infinitely through your days stuffing
yourselves with flowers and booze. You've filled your minds
with worry and sorrow for what may never come tomorrow.
You are no more than sick, and that death will be reborn,
unless you come with me to the summit of earth, the highest
peak, where you survive with your body, soul, and spirit
fused."

*

They've closed the gates. Full capacity. They all lie. The
guards have been ordered to create a yearning from the rest of
the public. Make them wait. Make them want more. Make
them envious of those who are short of tardy tendencies. The
Tall Fat Man has begun to take advantage of this conspiracy.

"Have some bread," he says to him and her and them and thee, "Bread made of dollars, bread of banks, broken bread from the bowels of Fort Knox." And as soon as he has arrived, is as long as he has slipped by the guards forced to hold the outside world at bay so the insiders could be the last of the elite; the lost and dying audience of the Minister.

*

"Your spirit waits for you upon the highest peak. If your spirit is there atop Eden, then your earthly vessel here is empty; your spirit is far from your usefulness. Your creator has separated you from yourself. Down here, on the greens, above the sea's level, you think you must search deeper, alone, within yourself to find salvation, to find Nirvana, a band that will never again write you another poem you have never understood. You believe verbal prayer will unify you, but only silence prevails. Your spirit yearns for you to silence yourself and to climb, alone, for that is what you all are— alone. Make mates for a month, one-night stands, birthing unwanted children, and blaming your baby's daddies. Your punishment is to climb, climb to a summit you will never reach. Climb to the heights where success dwells. There is nothing to admire down here below. There is no reward for an arduous climb with no end. Listen to me, and I will help you fly into a death that will open Its gates for you at the top, above the summit, below the stars."

*

A hulk sized male can barely stand, starved, weak in the knees, and he has fallen. His face pressed deep into the now, drowning in the soaked, muddy flooring of the greens; soaked from the salt of tears from the entire audience that collects their neighbors' porous residue into red cups, drinking the non-hydrating human water. The dusty dead grass has sprouted strands of green, nourished from the salted tears of this starved nation. The grass grows of empathy and creeps into the fallen strong man's lips. This should give him a reason to rise and yet, he does not gnaw. The salted sprouts are too bitter an herb to sit up for.

Something has changed. There is a new sound in the venue. A sound from days of old, competing with this Minister's babble. Someone has begun to strum a real electric guitar, stringing out Johnny B. Goode through a mobile speaker attached to his hip. "It's coming from that fat man," recognizes a young boy of twelve. He pulls upon this neighbor's shirt. Shoved to the side. No one can be bothered with childish rumors. They ignore the Fat Man. They all want to be entranced, hypnotized, emboldened into the Minister's cult. The Fat Man has no option but to, step by step and chord by chord, shove his bulbous body around the spiraling crowd, knocking every other brother down into the mud. The Fat Man seems to be on a mission to trample the missionaries.

*

The Minister is deaf and ultimately blind to others as he continues to speak his troubling word.

*

The Tall Fat Man begins to thin out, redistributing the indigestible goods he has stolen from the guards and retroactively begins to return the items to the fallen people. The crowd is thick, the Tall Fat Man needs assistance. He feeds the strong man first. From here to there the crowd is losing interest in the Minister as they find a tangible appreciation towards the Skinnier Fat Man. Is he tall? Was he short? Fat or Thin, this Man has begun to un-abduct this crowd from the intangible, contradictory rant of the Minister Con-Man at the podium.

*

And the Minister sneezed, and everyone said, "Bless you," and the Minister continued his word, as everyone returned their interest in the food their newest neighbor has brought them.

They have abandoned the Minister. They have left him ranting with threats and concerns the threats haven't been heard. The crowd has gone; dissipated and yet there will still be the downtrodden, the poor, the lonely, the haters, the fighters, the killers, and the thieves, but no one will be left behind upon the grass corresponding with the Minister as higher than thou. He is left with calm, peace, solace, silence, quiet, close your eyes Minister...

*

And now it was good.

*

The Short Bone Dried Man returned to his home North of the city, where temperatures were always below zero with no snow. He lived passed the projects, through the wind barrier of trees, along the highway lined with desolated motor-homes. A condominium, in a skyscraper designed by an independent contractor coerced by the glass, gas, and electric companies to build homes for the dying, was his home, with a view of the city. And this home was painted in rust.

Upon entering his beloved condominium, to his neutral reaction, found the heat and power had been turned off, the home had been gutted, and the windows broken through. Short Bone Dried Man makes his way to the door-less bathroom. Sits on the toilet, unrolls a sheet of inscribed TP and reads his memoirs.

*

In time, 89 more years to this day, he froze on his toilet, looking down at his feet that had trudged through the snow to the summit moments before. He remembered the final song he performed leaving the park behind, Carry on Wayward Son, only after leaving a joint upon the Minister's podium. The man, by error, or maybe by fate, yet unfortunately for himself, did just as the Minister had advised when he walked to the park and redistributed the traded goods. This giving man had reached his summit.

*

Now alone on his throne the Minister stood sad, unable to seek a mountain to climb, stranded on a plain, with a joint in hand and a match to strike—And the wind cries Mary.

#09

lonelier by the SEA

The wind is lonelier by the sea. There are no leaves. There are no petals. There is nothing of substance to brush upon. The wind can only toss fragments of stones among fragments on a beach. By the sea there are only birds that flock to their own agenda— survival. They will circle a current of cleaned clams. The birds will dive into the waters to catch a single fish—

                         Repeat until they are full.

        The seagulls are never full.

This is why he made the mile, foot by toe, to the last city to the shore each day. The clouds seemed to pass to quickly day to day, the moons would speed through the stars, the sun; a light.

Three hundred and thirty more years he was destined to live, while he continued to fill his lungs with the steadying green fumes of

.

.

.

history.

*

The gypsy from the south, dressed in soft linens and singing chains, would also come to the California shore. The sun warmed her right cheek into a rose, simmering into a tan line that slashed her face in two. The curves, maps of life that so romantically birthed from her eyes along her face, rolling her cheeks into a thing of bulbous beauty; cute. Her other face was as soft as a freshly powdered twenty-something with a life to live looking for love, still boisterous in the cheekers. She always wore her glasses. "Blind as a bat," she had told her newest friend.

"Maybe so, good for me, 'cause I can see you clearly," which ignited a blush on her tender side forever more, and beyond that time known to the infinite score.

*

As she walked along the waters, the shores of the ocean, the gusts of captivating, yet tender winds danced against her front and twirled along the crease of her back. She imagined the wind. Draped against her body like fabric. This is why she walked along the shore even though the sun burned her so. She wanted to seduce the wind in silence with simple bats of her blind eyes. She and her old friend concluded that it must be their age that has them thinking of the breeze so fondly.

*   *   *

There were and had been, still and quiet, two benches out yards from the rolling waters of the Pacific.

*

Moments sooner, forty steps or more, she repetitively places herself on the north bench and throws down tarot in rhythm to any song that might come to mind.

Thirty Six, Thirty 7, 38, 39, 40...

He passes her seat to take his own place on the south bench. Both made from the carve of fallen trees from the north pressed through a cement mold of one, two-piece, each operating as legs and as a back rest. He had designed them. He had designed a number of City cement items from benches to trashcans, barriers. He never made his own art. His art was for the city. So, as on every day of every year, he removed his shirt and turned his tanned self toward the kaleidoscopic sun rays burning out from the blanket of clouds and would say on cue, "Slow down, madam, the art of wishing will never get old."

*

Today he noticed his gypsy friend's hands had begun to tremble more often than usual. Her fingers seem to be stiffening. Her skin had begun to flake. The dryness of the southland desert shores had begun to wear this woman an awful something. To her, these were merely the haphazard trials of living a long life without children. Had she ever met a man worthy to conceive life? The tarot never told and so she must reshuffle the cards.

     He never spoke of the children he had never created. He cared for the gypsy. His silence was his way of showing his empathy for both of their misgivings. Their days together had grown fondly on him. He thought it would be better not to set into motion an awful reminder of their shared loss of innocence without infinite reward.

They had both loved before   they were sure of iT

They knew it to be truE

Both had to forget both paths to live into the future—

—a sure sign of love.

Yet,

he wondered each day if she would ever call upon him again as she did the very first day when she asked, "Would you like to dance?" That day they danced with the sea and he whispered to her ear, "It is the Ocean, the size mightier than any Sea," and each other.

From that dance on, she returned to throw tarot and hope to the imaginary Sea for an unsaid future. This puzzled him, as it would you, if your heart was challenged upon your return each passing day.

Who am I? He would wonder with eyes towards the infinite waters. He had forgotten himself so long ago, yet knew nothing of himself so very well. "I was transferred to work. I remember I wanted a son, but I don't recall, your name," he'd say to her on a number of occasions, as she continued to throw cards.

*

Today she did not show.

*

She was trembling the day after she returned. She had returned only a day late, late for consistency, pattern; he has drawn a blank. She was there, she always threw the cards. Now, as she was, she is there, across from me, throwing one, two, three to four cards, into the waves, so far, distant, on the other bench.

She was trembling. Her wobbly hands had increased in agitation and he asked, "Are you getting old without me?" and she spoke in return, "I'm afraid so, but you should stop smoking," and handed him a small Tupperware filled with herbal brownies. She had spent her absence preparing him a safer substitute for his inhalation of peace by the waters.

This was why her hands trembled more today—
She may have found love in her heart again.
Her baker's hands felt as so.

*

The sun began its retreat for the night.
*

Per usual, she rummaged through her bag of woven wheat and with shivers of trouble as she pulled out her precious tarot. "I rather not have your reading today," he said, staring out over the vast Pacific. He never cared for the future—

"Who cares to know what is to come if it cannot be seen, save for new lovers who yearn for a second sight," he commanded her in return for the gesture of tranquility, and the sour pain of trembling hands.

Throw a card and she'll lose her hands, forever, a sacrifice we cannot bear.

Burn the cards before they make him weep.

Steal them before she shuffles the deck.
Send me a postcard from Norway or Spain.
Don't draw the fool. She shuffles the deck.
Spills.
Do not bend for the unseen.
The waves, they'll sweep it away, you'll both be lost along the Ocean that leads to the Sea that leads to the sky into the peaks down the rivers and back to the lakes and the sea and the Ocean continues on. And the possibility was always terrifying. As the water grew near. Rumble, spill, slooooshhh...His life called for her to draw a...

...The beautiful gypsy in glasses sat in silence. The deck of cards shook between her brittle fingers. She began to draw them out of their cardboard box when he took her hand. He looked into this gypsy's dark eyes for the very first time; ah she has finally looked as well. "I love you," he said, and she looked upon him, forgetting her own eyes, feeling only the gaze of his soul. They saw each other's reflection, and she wept; years too long ago.

Today;
              "I am too old to love," she said in return as she tosses the remaining two cards into the sand, swoosh, stolen by the shadowed tide as another wave approaches. These are the shadows that can cover a building in the night and make requests of strangers to dance beside a bar to the ends of a bottle of gin. Flooded by the oncoming tide, the people are pebbles tumbling upon each other's lives, swept back out to see, confused with the—

—Single grains of emeralds and jewels soaked by the sea that
              slip into the sinkhole made by a single toe.

These are the grains of diamonds stolen from the fingers of widowed women and in this tinsel-town sooner will those rings slip from conjugal hands. Even the men are subject to theft—some by plastic and some by a stranger's thick dark eyes of a soul hung out on a fleeting truth, but a truth of nothingness nonetheless.

But wasn't that yesterday? It certainly was not today.

The sun is exhausted but will rise again tomorrow— on schedule in the hopes that its rays will waken them both, although one is a vampire and the other is a faceless clown.

*

The Fool and Death stare at the old man and his gypsy dream. They and these tricksters float farther and farther out into the near abyss of waters rolling miles from shore.

> Here is a hidden place in time
> where only the light of the lovely's eyes can be seen,
> and these two benched lovers
> miss the streaks of mist and heat
> streaks of fire soaring across the purple sky.
> They say it could be seen at the ends of Sunset Blvd.
> But there was no record ever found.
> No song.
> No one hit wonder.

*

Two planes, relics from the Sixties, Fifties, Forties, and every film in between, shoot towards the moon like soaring asteroids of fate. One plane so blackened by VIP speeds, so desperate for freedom, is a purchased streak resembling the mane of a mare in full stride / the other, a propeller, also VIP, carrying four, heading home from the ayahuasca meeting, back to the city life, behind the moon and into the moon. The planes collide behind the moon. She never saw it coming, the cards had been lost, the fire was without empathy, unknown, her love, blinded by the moon to the horror of the happening.

−_---x—z-czxcx-zxc---- The metallic wings instinctively curl into a twisted dance, spinning the bodies of insulated cabins in midair. Aluminum torsos melt from the fires ignited from fuel cells. The smoke of reefer from the backseats extinguished by the gust of air rocketing through the cabin, the aisle, at hundreds of miles per hour. The sound is that of an archaic army with the beat of their skinned drums. One hit, a thud so loud the thunder could be deafened, and the crumbling, the crackling, collapsing, sizzling, steamed, enflamed hydrogen, more blasts— Sparks; Metals upon Metals. Sizzling to a cool 55 degrees as it sinks deeper down the earth's Ocean's bottom. Some bones to follow, more ash distributed by the wind, swallowed by plankton.

"Have we always lived in LA?" he asked her. He could not recall, if he had been transferred into to town or across town. Was he always surrounded by the angels, he just couldn't recall?

*

Miles above the simmering ocean of sinking aircraft seatbelts and torn inflatable devices, the woman pilot reaches out her hand, curling her fingers around the intentional collision that occurred in this older man's bare and broken knuckles. She knows he has secrets, but the fall is too far, too short, too fast, she needs to hold on, even for just one night. They are survivors of the smoldering, will they be survivors of the fall, the submerging into the wavering Ocean below? The shards of glass slice at their feet, everything fluttering in the sky. Debris like bullets shooting into their flesh, their abdomens, lower backs, testicles, ovaries, arteries if they're lucky. Her mate lost in her eyes as they tumble, freely, enslaved by gravity.

The gypsy cleaned the lens of her glasses. Holds them up to the moon. They are clear. The Moon is full. The Ocean has swallowed the sorrow. The cards are nowhere in sight, just the full moon.

The old man shifts.

Takes a seat right beside her, on her bench, for the very first time.

Her hands tremble with the eye glasses in her fingers. He touches her skin, her knuckles, sliding his pruned fingers through, slipping the glasses from her hand, dropping them to the sand, and smashing them with his feet, "Now we are married."

"Why?"

The woman pilot turns one last time to her mate. A mile away from the break of the ocean. "I am too young to be alone this long," she said, kissed him as the current washed the old man away from the gypsy forever leaving her blinded by the lifetime of love lost in the Sea, the mass of waters she hadn't seen was the Ocean. And she ate the remaining brownies, and her hands began to steady, and her man returned from the Ocean, with treasures from the imaginary Sea.

#10

POT TOP
TOP POT
TTO PPO
OTT OPP
POT TOP

The top of the pot had been misplaced weeks ago. It was fine, it was a relic from boarding school. Used it a number of times to steam the shroom tea, other times to make weed butter, bake a cake in the dorm, serve it out to the second floor. The potheads lived on the second floor. The universe had created the Second Floor for weed. No one planned it, it just happened. You get roomed on the Second Floor, you're a pothead by second year, and there you stay. And there is where the rest of us get our weed, the Second Floor. I'm on the Fifth, my girl's in the building cross campus, my best buddy is on the seventh floor. My cousin's a Senior on the Second Floor. He hooks us up. Gives us the gram a day, a stash a week, seeds n' stems for shakes and smoothies, butter, and baking. We do all the Betty Crocker. We're over-weight, over-fed, and have an affinity for the finer things like hostess and Sara Lee. Just kidding, we're not fat, in fact most of us are relatively malnutrition from the cafeteria pizza as a preferred something flavorful choice besides Salisbury Steak and fries. That's Thursdays. I like Thursdays. I get extra baked on Thursdays.

*

Candice has a hardon for me. She's three doors down, crashing on Terry's floor. I laid Terry. I really liked Terry. She was down with droppin' and rustling through Central Park past 2am. Now Candice's asking about those nights. How was he? Does he get stoned to fuck, does he, go down stoned? I don't know, she's cool, attractive, but everyone's attractive around here, I just, she's, she's allergic to weed.

*

4am, still high from the gathering up at Columbia. Candice is leaning against my door. We've hooked up a number of times tonight. She's going to make this happen. "You sure you're allergic, or maybe it was just bad bud?"
   "I get hives."
   "Never heard of that?"
   "Do you have to have a girlfriend who smokes weed?"
   "I'm twenty-two, I can have a few girlfriends."
   "Not with me."
   "I respect that."
She's flattered. She likes him so.

                    I couldn't leave, we were at my door.
                       She's a committed lady, lay it all,
                          no middle ground, no one
                                             night
                                                st

                                                 a
                                                 n
                                                 d

                    I have to be myself, honest, true to me,
                               and that is true to all.
                    I make no judgement but upon myself.
                        Get my keys from my pocket,
                                    she's watching,
                                       going in?

I unlock the door, open it, step in, turn, "I'm sorry, I can't commit to a life without weed." She is sorrowed, true love swept off into the haze of a sadness that could write a thousand tragedies, for the man she loves is a boy she cannot have...but this is college, so she heads back to Terry's room, goes out the next night, falls in love with a killer guy who prefers smoking opium to weed, and common chill-ground is romantically found in the face of rejection.

*

As for me, I moved to Colorado.

#11
THE
KEY
TO
CALM

I blame the flip-flops. Never been fond of flip-flops; on guys, anyhow. I won't wear Birkenstocks either 'cause a sandal's just a heftier flip-flop.

The Purist, "In fact the sandal is the predecessor of the Flip-Flop."

So is eating poison berries to cyanide...

The Chemist, "Well—

Here's my point. You won't catch a Drag Queen sporting flip-flops out in public until she's on the sand. Not in NY anyhow. I do have a pair I use in the gym's showers. I fear the flesh-eating disease squiggling under my already dead toenails—Yet as of late I have a second reason for the rubbery, free flapping, slip on footwear. I have succumbed to a reason to flip the flap upon the sidewalk.

Flip— Flap. Flip— Flap. Flip—

Southern California's been victim to a serious heat wave since July. Averaging 88-90 degrees on the west side, ocean side. There is no breeze. I've taken up aimless walks along the Santa Monica beach, mid-day, 3 - 5pm, where I sit my ass on a bench to write stories into my phone.

Flip— Flap. Flip— Flap.

This new hobby sucks in shoes. Yesterday I sucked up my pride and fashioned the flip-flops, so I didn't have to carry my Docs forever as I trudged through the sand. If you've never walked the Santa Monica side North of the Pier, where they shot Bay Watch, it is not a casual stroll from the pavement to the water line. That's a five-minute trudge. You don't do that in shoes to be relaxed, and that sand is running at about 150 degrees, so you don't do it barefoot.

Flip— Flap. Flip— Flap.

The flip-flop curls over the miniature hills of the dotted beach. Boots press down hard, dig, pulls the sand back out with a step; trudge. The flip-flop, curls, presses, sure, but doesn't dig in, you are almost barefoot without the burn, or the shard of broken glass digging into the arch of your foot.

Flip— Flap. Flip— Flap. Fl-p. Water. Tide. Wet sand.

I string the black flip-flops through my belt. Another convenience. Boots pull my shorts down, too heavy, have to hang 'em over the shoulder, around the neck, but that's nasty. The flip-flops string like a feather hanging from my leather belt.

I walk hands free.

My playlists converse with me through the ear bud; PCH side.
Cuts out the mechanical waves;
The West ear, free to listen to nature's waves.

I've sold myself on the flip-flops.
Within the first hands free walk I was a complete convert.
I have now put my faith in this new freedom of the feet.

*

Today, like most, I have driven the 20 plus blocks from my abode to Ocean Blvd. LA lazy. It's a thing. Not a joke. Live here long enough and you're a fucking slave to the roll. No matter, I'm not that much of a douche bag, I roll the pavement with reason; if I walk the whole twenty-blocks, instead of the drive, then I lose the will, through projection, to tackle the repetitive windy flights of stairs tearing at your tired thigh strands each and every step, destroying all that the end of the world of peace had to offer, and that can be LA, if you don't figure a way, so I drive, save the thighs, give the climb a nothingness, a no matter. To be clear, after walking 20+ blocks, you still have to walk down 100+ steps to sea level, which equates to having to climb 100+ steps to even start going home. It's exhausting.

All those Suburban peops out in the plains of Oklahoma don't realize that about the prettier side our sea line, Santa Monica, where Pamela gave her jiggle in a red swimsuit every week...It's a hike if you don't go the mile South to enter at the Pier...anywhere else, a hike of a thousand stairs, and an overpass cross the PCH, highway numero Uno; that's Spanish for number one.

-----~*

I hit my faithful Jetty Extract pen, turn off the SUV, breathe, sigh of nothingness, a cruise so clear, no red lights, no pedestrians crossing unstop crosswalks, and a trust in my life rules.

      *   *   *

Rule numero zero—
Never leave the house without a fully charged vape pen or at least one rolled spliff, doobie, joint, blunt, etc...

      *   *   *

"Liberating,"
I say to myself from the rearview mirror
Process. I need my wallet, my headphones, my phone— shit I got too much in my hands, "Put these down," I say and drop something and remember, FLIP-FLOPS!— It's too hot in the 4Runner. Like 98 outside. LA's on fire. Smoldering with the windows up. Got my mind mixed up— Open the door. Fucking humid as hell out there? Why is it humid in So. Cal? ~~~~~~~~~~~~~~~~~~~~~~~~~~~~~~~~~~'A slight breeze sneaks through the open door, but not really, not enough. I wipe the sweat from my eyes. Bend over, start to unlace my boots. Docs are a fast off, forever to put back on. I toss the ox blood pair in the back, unroll my socks, wet, smell 'em like a dog, we're all dogs, gotta get a wiff, just checking things out, intellect fails, instinct kicks in, nasty, gag, ditch those farther

in the back...they're going to fester in the sun back there, lovely, and grab the...where the fuck are the Flip-Flops? Mutha Fucka, I can't find them.

I'm tossing my helmets around the back seat. I've let the skullcaps pile up in the recent month. I go out too much. When did I stop watching TV? I used to watch TV to take the pain away...now I go out to meet the world instead. Outside. In LA. There is nothing to do in LA. There are things to do, but people don't dance at bars. I'll settle for going to the beach in boots under the moon to get my dance on. At least on the vast shore when I'm the only one dancing at my bar in my hand, it's because I am the only one there, me, mean steam, and me. I just have to be outside lately. Maybe it's the humidity. Maybe it's the whiskey and weed? Fuck, I can't find my dumbass flip-flops anywhere. This is a travesty. I squiggle through the front seats grasping for my boots on the floor. I gotta put my boots back on. So hot. I might have to pee. I do. String the laces. One lace, two hole, nother lace, leave two eyes open, wrap the leg, once, twice, tye 'em up, double knot, next foot. Too hot to turn back now. I'll tread the sands of Santa Monica.

Rule number one—
Never leave your weed in the car.
Reason: If you lose your car, it gets stolen, destroyed, or you're a total loser and you lose your keys, at least you got your weed.

This rule is imperative for all safe, calm travels. If you leave your weed in the car and your car gets stolen, you will have no weed to smoke. That is an Uncomedy. That's when you find grown men weeping on the side of the road. There is nothing funny about your weed being stolen, especially when your car has been jacked.

-----~*

I sweep the Jetty Pen outta of the cup holder, sip a pip, slide it in my back pocket, hop the fuck out, lock the door from the inside— I left the car clicker at home, it snapped off the key ring, plastic broke, can't attach it nothing, free-balling car clicker— don't want to lose that clicker in the sand, know what I'm sayin? I did that unwritten rule unconsciously today. Rule worthy instinct.

Rule number 1.2—
Do not take free-balling car clickers to the beach in your pocket; ever.

o o o o   o   o o o OOoO O OOOO OOoooooo—And I'm out, *Lou Reed* in the earbuds, one street to cross (Ocean), and I take the massive slabs of drift wood steps down with ease, no care, I didn't walk here, and I'm over PCH, around the downward spiral staircase, easier to skip down, then step up, and you're across the billion dollar a minute parking lot— bam freedom, beach world, peace, no pressure. *"Vicious," says Lou, "You hit me with a flower..."*

*

I walk north up the bike path towards the Palisades. "There's a boardwalk just up ahead," I tell two college girls lugging two bags each, an umbrella, with their flip-flops curled in their manicured bling sprinkled fingernails. They think I'm hitting on them, smile, and say, "That's okay"—LA girls— They think everyone talks from the dick here— I blame the fat cat producers for that. I see no couch on the beach. What's the big?

     I do look a bit like a porn producer with my trusty rooster head trucker's hat, pho-cop sunglasses, strutting with a dance in my step, shirtless absorbing some sun to kill the tan line I got. Maybe they shouldn't talk to me? But I'm one of the nice ones— I'm just a writer with style and holes in his jeans. Maybe it's the flip-flops? No. I got boots on today. Must be the sunglasses. Fuck 'em, they can trudge through that sand.

Another five minutes, a song and a half later, and I make a cut early today, walk the plank walkway to the benches nearer to the actual shoreline.

*

The benches are free. There are two benches here. If you read my Lonelier by the Sea story you kind of know what I'm talking about— aka the benches were not fiction, just the characters and actions, and I never saw the plane crash, but I read about it the next day—

I sit my ass down on the north end bench. Hot as fuck out here. No breeze. No clouds. No shade. I'm just going to lay on the bench instead. Close my eyes— Fade away into the music in one ear and the ocean in the other. Fend the fire. Jerk off into the sky; in another life.

*

No one has called or texted for the past hour I've laid here with the Eagles of Death Metal, Zepplin, Cream, some Magnetic Fields, Fugazi, The Who, NoMeansNo, Mayfield, Love, Alice Donut, Underworld, some early Pixies. I sit up. "An hour?" crack my back, "I should walk"—Sip, sip, the Jetty pip; ipe.

*

The sun drops earlier and earlier as October rolls along. Last week it was still centered over the expanding ocean. You were still able to make out some of the green colors of the Santa Monica waters. This is not the Caribbean. Let's not fool ourselves, but there is still beauty in destruction. Destruction allows for new things. I'm not so sure that truly works for the water though. We all came crawling from the sea— Sulfur levels making life. Probably not the earth womb we should be fucking around with, if you catch my drift. Leave that lady alone. Swim in her. Love her. Kiss her. Lick her hidden sulfur tubes— submerge in her beauty, but stop shoving beer bottles, and plastic straws up her ass. That shit just ain't cool. Garbage will ruin her for years to come. I guess because the sun has moved northwest its reflective powers no longer create a green tint in the sea. The water is a molten metal instead.

Rolling tides that glisten in the final rays of the fire in the sky. You can see the moon if you look south. You can see Aliens along the Seattle sea shore. This is not Seattle. All our Aliens are Scientologists down here.

*

I continue my walk north along the wet sand. Every third wave and I have to dance away from the tide because I totally left my flip-flops at home and do not want to carry my boots and mess up my chill. I never wrote today. I wasn't feeling it. I call the sea my mistress. Second only to my apartment. The city's just a slut-whore who'll taunt and tease and make you pay for the bill— then fuck the bartender instead and get a free drink next week —The sea is more reliable with crashing waves that are much less predictable. Furious fodder for the brain. Easy undertows for the heart.

   The birds are crazy for fish today. They dive, five, six at a time around a family of people that play in the crashing waves. These Angelinos don't seem to care about the birds' late lunch. They think it's cute. I wouldn't trust those birds. They're like spears with brains. Hungry brains. They should really get out of the water. I'd yell shark, but that ain't cool.

*

Okay I gotta turn around. I've walked thirty minutes farther than ever before. I'll be in the Palisades if I keep this up. My wallet's not thick enough to be caught half naked on a Palisade beach. Besides, if not a young one, then it'll be a Cougar with a cash call and as much as I could use a free dinner or two, the price is way too high. What if a lady on the hill falls in love with me? I'm too honest to put up with that. I turn around— These are the thoughts of this writer. This is what I have to put up with. Me, myself and the strangeness that finds me throughout my lifetime. I put up with him. I do his work for your entertainment. I can sense her looking my way. From her cliffside homestead window. Her eyes shine in the street light that has prematurely turned on for the evening. Her nose twitches. Smells. My sent, it has been hot, my aura is no more than the mist of my body odor. She steps out onto her balcony, I turn, she finds another down the shore. Not as lean as I. Walking with his vulnerable female. I step faster. I will fend the waters if need be to distance myself from her prowl as she vanishes from her perch, gone into the trees, cross the PCH, I look back, she's taking the female human by the neck, offers the meat to her lover, he can't resist as he bends to his knees beside them both, feasting off the breast meat of his dead ex-fiancé. "But now I have nowhere to live," he says to the cat licking her paws clean of his past. "Prrr, you'll stay with me," she curls up against his leg, pats his member, "Up on the hill...I have another car if you need."

*

Okay the sun's going to sleep, sooner than later, and I'm getting a little hungry. Peckish. Oh, the stomach growled. Hello belly. Maybe some steak and eggs from *Norms*. You like that? Grrrr. Don't worry little fella you'll be a happy tum-tum soon enough. I hit the Jetty. Stoned free. Grrrrr. Ah shut up. Gotta pee. Do that now; public bathroom by the parking lot. Pee before you walk the hill of hell steps. Hate to touch the doorknobs. Worse is the lock on the inside. That's the post potty knob. No sink in there and never much TP. What the fuck? Fail in design. LA politicians were tired of explaining herpes to their spouses so they figure contaminate the entire public and we're all on even footing, mouthing? Good for the people. I barely touch the door handle to open it. Ugh, now I have to lock the door from the inside and touch my dick. I use my index and thumb for the deadbolt. I'll use the pinkies to hold the Pee-pee. I ain't catching nothing in the Gym. I ain't catching something from the beach bums. Okay, pee done, wash hands, hike back up the massive spiral stairs to the PCH overpass, over the PCH, up the wooden mountain stairs to Santa Monica ground level, then get to the car and gets me some food. I 'll take it slow. First, out of this john.

-----~*

I'm mellow. I'm hitting the Jetty as I take one step at a time.

Puff, step, puff, step, step, puff, and step. I used to take the steps fast. Dumb. Take them slow like a tourist and it makes for a stress less summiting back up to civilization. *Jane's 's Addiction* takes me home. *Nothing's Shocking*. Back to the city? Back to the strip-mall landscape. Maybe I should go to strip-club tonight? A funny one.

*

I reach my 4Runner. I think I'm going call my drive *The Shadow*. I'm done with the music that blares in my head. I drop the ear-buds into my front pocket, swipe the lock screen, dump instagram, go to dump the playlist, but I get a text from a new acquaintance, "What's up?" — "Nothing." The end. Not in the mood to write author paragraphs to my various friends who'll only ask me if I'm going out or where they could get some illegal drugs— typewriter sound —another one blows up my phone—

"You know where I can get some Acid?"—
"Don't ask illegal shit on my phone. Especially in TEXT!"—
"You hangin?"
"No."
"U know about systemic ecosystems?"
"Gotta go."

You have to be careful texting a writer. We write. Texting is a portal to our intellectual climax. It's what we do. Write. Read. Cum. Write. Read. Pee. You'll only get a Yes or a No if it fits the story or if we know we can't be disturbed. If I respond with a brief thought on this, I'll be leaning up against the Shadow for the next 20 minutes crafting text after text of philosophical mumbo jumbo with my feet in the fucking street and not sitting on a stool at Jumbos. Any other time and this unsuspecting texting victim would have to suffer through my thoughtfully crafted novellas and poetry in text because writers think text is a place, we can be poets without any real judgment. Text is not the place. We do it none-the-less. We're the highly acclaimed most obnoxious humans to use language. Love us or hate us.

Do not text a photographer. You are bound to only get picts and stupid memes in return, "A picture says a thousand words." Well a thousand words is either too much or not enough. What does a filmmaker do? Probably ignores the text because they have to hire a cinematographer, gaffer, screenwriter, and an actor to talk for them. Besides, the executive producer of the text is going to make the director change the ending anyway. Hit the Jetty and open the door, but the car door don't open. My 4runner is not opening. What the fuck? Oh shit, 'cause it's locked. Ha, I'm so stoned.

Where the fuck are my keys?

Pat down all my pockets. No fucking way. Pat them again. Dig those hands in there Mutha Fucka. Dig. No! There are no fucking keys. Where the fuck are my keys?! I look toward the sea. Oh mother of G-d. Did they fall when I passed out on the bench? In the sand? My nightmare, my rules. Please no. It's getting dark. Check the pockets. Oh, hello Jetty. And I take a hit. Rule Number Uno. Least I got my weed. I look through The Shadow's tinted windows. Do I see them? No, too dark in there. Use the phone flashlight. The light just reflects back from the windshield. This is fucked. Come on, they have to be in there. I don't see them. I'd see a shine off the metal keys by now. No time to waste. Sun is almost gone. I have to get back to that fucking bench!

*

I'm glad I don't smoke pot anymore. I know, travesty. How could Tzvi say such a thing?! Fuck you. I hit my Jetty Cannabis Oil all day every day and I am a much better person, artist, and breather for it. I don't cough in the morning anymore and I'm not going to vomit my lungs out after hustling down those Santa Monica steps. Okay get to the bench. Run, Mutha Fucka, Run! Do not fall.

*

Back at the bench. It's dusk dark. Nearly impossible to see

anything clearly. The phone light isn't strong enough, but I'm shining it all over the place for effect. There are plastic planks under the benches. If the keys were here, they'd be here. I'm on my hands and knees to push around some of the sand behind the bench. Maybe some brat or drug addict kicked them into the sand for no reason other than absolute obnoxiousness. They're not here. Where did I lay down? Is my imprint still there? Nope. Somewhere over here. I gently kick the sand around, reveal nothing. I'm on my knees brushing the sand away. If I dig I may not feel them. Feel them. Please.

Honestly, I hope they're not here because I cannot find them anywhere. They better be in my car. Maybe under the seat? Hit the Jetty. Ah, mellow out. You still have your weed, Tzvi. Good boy. Follow those rules. Add keys to your rules. Never thought I'd have to do that. Kind of figured that was a total given. Not today.

*

Call your neighbor. I gave Violet a set of house keys for an emergency. At least I can go home. Holy fuck, my phone only has 8% of its battery life left. That sucks. "Violet! Holy shit balls, listen, it's Tzvi," I yell into my cell.
    "Oh, I'm in a hurry. Is everything okay?" she asks, but I cut her off.
    "LISTEN! I need my house keys. I locked myself out of my car. Can you pick me up?"

                                        No response.

    "Hello?" I ask.
    "My dog's going berserk. Can I call you back? Thanks sweetie," she says—

"No! FUCK WAIT! KEYS! LEAVE MY KEYS!"

I think she heard me. She hasn't hung up yet.
    "Violet?"
    "MUSTER!" I hear her scream on the other end of the phone

and then it goes dead.

                                        She better had heard me.

    *   *   *

My legs are chugging through the sand, gotta run, gotta get
home. Hit the pavement, run, run mutha fucka, run...to the
stairs. The stairs. I'm at the bottom of the spiral, the steps
across the PCH, they get higher and higher the longer I stare.
This will be the challenge of a lifetime, I must run, and
continue to run. Breathe, run. Breathe...

    R   U   N

                                                  R

                              U

              N

RUNrunrun,steps,somanysteps,run,palmspressureagainstthig
h,longstep,palmspressureagainstthigh,up,longstep,
twenty more? Go, Tzvi, go...

...last step, I'm gonna die, the lights green, fuck, take it, don't
stop, roll with the inertia, get across Ocean Ave, on the
asphalt, halfway, flashing red hand, still green, onto the
sidewalk, go, man, go, I'm going to die, did I really take those
steps, so fast, both ways, so fast, past my car, look again? no
get home, get home, get the clicker first, just in case, get the
mutha fucking clicker before Violet gets Muster in the car. Go
man go, go, go...

...I hightail it the first 6 blocks. Fireballs of hell spill from my
heels, Lincoln, greenlight again, got that on my side, up the
block, past the grocery, past the bank, up, up Montana, keep it
up, up, up, I stop at the Duck Blind. I need some whiskey.

———————————————————————————————————————

"I got the weed. That, I didn't lock in my car," I vent to the liquor store bartender; the loyal cashier.

"But you need some whiskey?" he asks.

"No, I'd just like some whiskey. And this water. I didn't lose my wallet, and see," I display my pen, "Still got my weed. No time to cry, yet."

"Those good?"

"Fantastic, probably legal in a couple years. The whiskey's for when I get home, home. Like car home."

I immediately down the whole water.

"If you find the keys let me know," he says. "Sure thing. Thanks for the talk," and I run again.

The longer it takes for me to understand how screwed I am, the longer tonight will be if the car keys are totally gone. No, I don't have a second set of those. Don't judge me. That's like $350 bucks. Fuck that. I lost the other pair. My friend lost the other pair. In Portland, he thinks. Still got my clicker— at home —I gotta start running again. It's a red light. Green and I'm off, then it's red light after red light after red light, then when I'm drifted, waiting impatiently, it turns green, and I pop right into the obstacles that populate a street of shopping, design, hair, and coffee. Some yuppie in a four-door, gold Porsche is California rolling the stoplight to go right. He's texting as well. He almost kills me as I throw myself in front of two housekeepers with strollers and infants. I slam my fists against his precious $25,000 hood with a fury, "Go fuck yourself! You murderous text junky!" Then I turn to the housekeepers to explain, "Probably making an online appointment for his Tantric session." Turn, bump into a barista on a break, spilling his only free coffee for the day, and I'm running again. I have to get home. I cannot be distracted again— And then came the banana.

I never saw it.
     Totally blindsided in the boot.
          It was sneaky.
               Just sprawled out on the sidewalk. Each peel stretched out like a starfish. I didn't see it until I took flight. I had been cursing the golden Porsche douche bag when the truck of bananas lost control at the wheel. I never saw the truck crash directly into the Aero Theater as I raced up the sidewalk. There were hundreds of nearly ripe bananas slung into the evening sky. Green and yellow wingless fruit. I slipped. I don't know how far or for how long I was in flight, but I sure was high.

High enough to see hordes of flying purple elephants soar out from the dark fog layer. Bat like wings hold their hefty bodies in the air as they use their trunks to scoop up single bananas and toss them in the sky.

          High enough to watch the purple skinned pachyderms catch the fruits one by one in their mouths and return to scoop up another and another.

High enough to see the flamenco mermaid-clown

dancers pole slide on the
streetlights and pose for
the ticket cams with their
tails spread out. And I
wonder how a mermaid
spreads its tail like that?

High enough to
compare the color of the night sky with the
glittering lights of the movie theater that blind the
blind men that sell pencils on the rooftops.

Long enough to laugh myself into oblivion
under the triple layered top hat with a
skeleton in a fake beard performing a
sermon on the rim— Long enough for me
to tear off the hipster's beard and tell him to
grow some on his balls.

Long enough to sing sadder songs about
the funny fool who takes sips of soda
pop with an apricot dwarf that blows
bubbles in my ear. Flipping pantomime
in spirals with dancing toes and
sulfur hoes. I can't see my
mistress the sea as she is covered
in the dark night even from way
up here.

Long enough to
soar past folly's
with   black,
leopard skinned,
pregnant   boas
that sell hearts
of glass to my
former   self
'cause,   "I'm
invisible like a
razor of love"—

And I realize my
playlist   hasn't
stopped.

Long enough to check my battery. 2%. I hope I get home.

Long enough to hit the Jetty two more times.

Fast enough to race the sporadically U-turning double you-s and grand standing VW's against the Venice beach hydro-monster cars that surf along the curl of fog blanketing the rooftops of Santa Monica while the hippies in the graveyard across town wave peace signs in protest of a world without absolute peace because they are already dead.

Just slow enough to dip my fingers into a rainbow dream and smear the sky with majestic oils. Passive enough to watch my sky transform into a kaleidoscopic eyeball that blends into a kiss and imprints itself on our psychedelic pupils of infinite space.

Just slow enough to see there is another soul that your very own soul has and infinitely so. Just slow enough to be alone with all your other selves. Just slow enough to know it's not enough to see so far if you cannot see what is fluttering before your face, the mite, tossed into the air as well, thrown from his home on your two week unwashed jeans. Far enough to miss my own hands. Deep enough to forget my legs. Long enough to grow wings—To prevent my fall. To continue my crawl. To scratch my own balls. To piss the useless goals away. To focus on the darker gold liquid that is the Cannabis Oil along the way,

home.

Just slow enough to land on my feet with the bending of a knee, three steps back, three steps forward, and thank you G-d and please get me home. But life is adversarial. So, I hit the Jetty weed stream once again and skip a rock over the catastrophe that is the ruckus of battling purple elephants who use their tusks to tear each other down to dominate the feed of the last few bananas. "You all just gotta chill. Smoke some weed," I say as I hoof it past the pachyderms—

—but
elephants don't smoke weed, or vape for that matter— so all for not. I got seven more blocks to go. "If the devil is six, then the G-d is seven," said *Black Francis* on the beach when I found peace and tranquility in the eyes of the sea. Eons ago, and

agone.

*

I flip my neighbor's doormat. "I'll leave the keys under the mat," was the last text I got before I hit that banana. I tried to respond back with a thumbs-up emoji, but the 2% of phone battery died out as quickly as I swiped unlock— Yes, the house keys are here. I can get into my place.

*

I gotta pee. Clicker first. Grab that. Slip that into my change pocket of my jeans. There it will live safely. Wait. There's a hole in these jeans, right? Shit. Yup a pocket hole. Oh fuck, charge the phone. Right here. The charger is right beside me. Plug that in. Good. Charge bitch. Change my pants. I gotta pee. Pee first. I already dropped my jeans. Okay scoot to the john with the *Levis* around your ankles. Almost trip. Catch myself against the dresser. I'm going to die like this one day. Shoot the pond. Losing weight. Feeling better. Give me a moment. I gotta breath. It's dark out. Night is so here. No keys in the car will mean I'm waiting hours for a tow. I saw the street cleaning sign. I have to move that car before 8am. I have to get it towed tonight. Then what? I'll have to wait 'till tomorrow to buy a new key. How long will that take? Tow a car twenty blocks. Sounds so lame. I should just push it. Fuck! Can't push a car you can't automatic shift into neutral. Ugh! Hit the Jetty. Hit the J-E-T-T-Y. Think positively. Smoke more then pull your pants up. I think I gotta pee again. Yup. Twinkle, twinkle little star. I can see a single star through my bathroom window. Night is fucking here. Shake it off. Get back to the car bro.

*

I've pissed. I've checked my pocket. I have the car clicker. Okay, house keys? Fuck where'd I put my house keys. Get a fucking grip, man. I hit the Jetty. They're on the bookshelf. Jetty eyes. That's what I call clarity. I never leave keys on the bookshelf— Maybe if you didn't smoke so much, wrong. Flip-Flops are to blame. Maybe I have to pee again? No. I'm cool. Just go. So, clicker— check. House keys— check. Jetty— hit it. So good. Okay I'm kind of having a good time again. Hilarious. This shit is dramatically hilarious in my crazy brain. Maybe I should take the acid in my freezer. Nah, I'm saving that for the right time. Now is not that time. I've returned to myself. Laugh it off. Laugh at that. Laugh at the life in which we weave— Sweating like a mutha fucka. Still 85 outside. Probably 90 in here —Switch shirts— I only have four varieties of shirts. I have Black T-shirts, black colored Polo/Izods, two to three black button ups, and a myriad of black muscle undershirts. I have other kinds, but more or less this set is what keeps me thinking instead of deciding— I got to get out of my head —I go Polo. I have a thing for making yuppie wear go the punk way. Take the piss out of their reality. I really got to find my car keys. I got fifty thousand blocks to walk again. At least I don't have to do the beach stairs for a sixth time. Or do I? Not if the keys are in the car. Okay, lights, door, got my keys, check, get the fuck out of here.

*

CLICK—BEEP, BEEP—My car unlocks. I open that door in a fury. I find the car keys in between the seats. I sit. I drop my head against the steering wheel from pure exhaustion. I weep. I laugh. I curse the day. I love the new night. I blame the Flip-Flops. Flip-Flops make the world go flippity-flap. That shit is annoying. Today the rubbery slip on footwear crossed the line. They didn't follow me to the beach. They ditched me. Stayed home in the gym bag. They confused me. They rattled my brain with their flip-flop attitude about stability. At least I never left my weed in the car and had charged my Jetty pen before I ever left the house in the first place. Rules are not always meant to be broken. Shit, where'd I leave my phone?

#12
HAZY, LAZY, *n'* CRAZY

There was no exit off this futon. The studio apartment billowed in smoke. The hallway reeked of marijuana— It was only noon o'clock —There was no way these three stoners would be going outside today. Maybe if they smoked another bowl? "It's always worth a try," someone says aloud. "What's worth a try?" says another male voice. "Going outside," the original voice answers. A young woman's hand adorned in rustic jewelry sways the smoke away from her tender, rainbowed haired face. Her lipstick matches her hair. Her eyebrows drawn-in per mood, today they are white. "He wants to smoke another bowl," she informs the remaining clouds. The fog begins to dissipate from one of the males. "Don't pack it so tight this time," insists the longhaired, newborn millennial hippy with a few dreads and a raggedy spider trailed beard. "Chill man. I'll get it good," the urbanized peacock street hippy in a Hindi skirt with a long sleeve, hole infested t-shirt stamped on the back with a faded black & white illustration of a pot leaf haired Jesus on a dabber cross with a doobie sticking out of the savior's side.

"Where'd you get that shirt?" the baldhead to her right asks while tracing the lines around the doobie in the messiah's belly.

"I just got it," the Peacock answers with a shrug, "Come on guy. Yer kinda fucking up my grind."

"Testy," penis top slips back into the futon, covering his circumcised college skull cap with his black hoody, and sulking.

Who invited her he first place?
She'll come around.
We'll bang by tonight.

He was just so stoned. The Hippy always forgot about the Bald One. The Hippy always preferred hanging with the Peacock. Hippy almost got with her on Molly in March, now it's July, and July means you can see his bulge 'cause he's gotta wear star moon glory hole button up skin tight boxer shorts so he don't slip out of his normal shorts. Hippy's hung. Fact's a fact and he knows it. Peacock knows too. Peacock knows he knows. So, she looks him in the eye and grinds the weed in her palms, back and forth, back and forth, pissing off the teeter tot turtle in a hoody...he's trying to keep the bulge at a minimum...and no, Peacock is not going to get with him, and he never even almost got with her in the first place. He asked if he could crash in her bed after the party, she said, "no," he went and slept down the hall. In the morning, she sold him some weed and told him he was a total gentleman for sleeping in the hall and that she'd never forget it. He bought a quarter from her, to add to the eighth she sold him in the doorway last night before he asked to crash. Peacock's done grinding the bowl.

ooOOOoo

They never cleared the bong. Smoke still twists itself out of the glass tube. The bong smoke smells stale. A dirt to the burn. Peacock grinds that shit some more. Back and forth, back and forth. Left then right. She cranks the metal top open. "All resin in there, man. Clean that shit. Gets jammed up," and she pops it back on and back and forth, left then right. "Yeah, I gotta clean that," the Hippy agrees. The Bald One mopes. "I just thought it was a cool shirt," he says under his breath. "Crawl back in the womb dude," she says knocking his knee with hers. "Yeah whatever," the Bald One pouts.

"We're gonna give him the first hit, kay?" she says to the Hippy as she stomps the shredded weed out onto the folded printer paper.

"Right on that. Cheer up the guy," the Hippy agrees again.

"I can hear you guys," the Bald One is morphing into an annoying little brat for no reason 'cept being totally in love with the Peacock who could care less if he was on a ledge pledging all his love to her with a gun against his dick. "Shoot it. That would be crazy," she would say. And she'd imagine that this fetus of a man boy, would probably actually do it, and shoot his own dick off for her. And she'd be right.

"You really gotta mellow out dude. You want to hit this or what?" she asks him as she bangs the debris from the bong stem into the ashtray and gently packs the next bowl. "You gonna clear it first?" he asks back— Wow, what a tight wad — "Yeah man. Whatever," and she clears the bong from the stale smoke and sucks down the pain, exhaling it right into his hood hole. "That shit smells vile!" he gasps, gags, spit on the carpet. "Classy, guy," Peacock chirps. "Fuck off," says the smallest of men, who deserves no such treatment...Unless, he was a handsy mutha fucka that night.

ooOOOoo

The Bald One sits up.
Cracks his neck.
Takes the bong.
Peacock is willing to light it for him.
He takes the lighter from her,
"I can do it. I'm not a child."

x o x X x o x

—Leaning over to the Hippy, Peacock simply says, "No, he's a fucking infant,"—"I can still hear you"—"Hit it already!"

The Bald Brat grimaces at and hits the bong. They watch as he takes the whole tube with one long inhale. His eyes fill with clouds. His nostrils leak a stream of smoke. His face; red. His lungs hold the evaporated ash deep inside. They wait for him to exhale. Will he ever let it go? Might pass out. What is he trying to prove? Nothing. He's just stupid and lets it all out followed by a cough that lasts a good couple of minutes.

Cccccccccccc   Cccccccccccc   Cccccccccccc

Cccccccccccc Cccccccccccc   Cccccccccccc

Cccccccccccc   Cccccccccccc   Cccccccccccc

Peacock is not impressed. The kid sinks back into the futon. She points out that there's a little something at the corner of his lip. He wipes away the dribble from the cough attack. She laughs at him. A cackle sort of laugh. Like a chicken in heat.

Why pick on me?
Why you gotta be like that?
I'm just hanging out.
Why you gotta be all bitch flirty?

The Bald One whimpered and cried to himself behind his mystique of anger that could only be described as the pout of perfection.

    The Hippy's bored of the futon and suggests, "Maybe we should make a gravity bong?"

"Hell yeah," Peacock's in and whacks the Bald One in the ribs.

"I thought we were going outside?"

The Hippy gets up to fetch a gallon water tub. "My knees cracked," he announces, and Peacock just looks at him like, "*So?*

"Doesn't generally happen."

"So?"

"Just saying."

"Tub."

The Bald One has slouched deeper into the futon. He's watching Peacock out of the corner of his eye. He wants her. He is a tiger with no paws, no teeth, no hide; hidden. She doesn't notice him. She isn't going to notice. "You want to hook up?" he asks, just loud enough for her to know he actually said that shit. "No."

"Why not?" he begs.

"Cause you're lazy," she says shooing his leg away from her.

He feels rejected.

She gets up.
Whoa,

kinda

stoned.

She adjusts the peacock like feathers of hair that flare out of her scrunchy. "Gravity bong boner. Come!" she commands and stumbles her way to the bathroom. Peaks in. The Hippy is melting a metal bowl into the plastic cap for the gallon jug. "Could you cut that?" he asks her elbowing towards the jug. "Scissors?"

"I don't know. Find some?"

"Lame dude."

He ignores her, continues to melt the cap away while the water gushes into the bath, and the Bald One pops up behind the pretty bird spooking her.

"What the fuck man? Creepy."

"That gonna be the gravity bong?" asks shit shine.

"Yeah duh. Find me some scissors," she commands the testicle wimp of a stoner dude who was lame enough to ask if he could hook up, but he doesn't move, "Please?" she whines with her vagina eyes trying to talk in a language the Bald One might understand.

"Yeah okay."

ooOOOoo

Peacock sits it down on the john. Her knees spread wide, the hippy Hindi skirt drapes between her thighs, fanning out from her bare feet on the tiled floor. "What's with that guy?" she asks the Hippy. "What's with anyone really?" — "Turn the water off dude," she says as she cranks the faucet closed, "I just got accepted into early enrollment."

O

The Hippy looks up from the finished cap-bowl. "Marines?" he asks. She whaps his half dreadlocked head, "College man."

"Useless knowledge," the Hippy quotes Bob Dylan.

"You smoke too much weed dude. Why you quotin' that shit?"

"I got scissors," says the man-child with eager beaver pecker balls. Peacock swipes the shears and picks up the plastic jug. Out of the corner of her eye she looks over at the Bald One, jabs the open scissor into the lower belly of the plastic jug, twists, smiles and exclaims, "Oooh. Hot huh."

Yes.

Bald Job doesn't flinch. "Go get the weed," she instructs him. And he does as she says.

ooOOOoo

All three of these brains of tomorrow are on their knees. They are preparing to take the *Eucharist* of bored stoners with nothing more to do than smoke more weed in various shapes, forms, functions, and what-evers.

"Thank you green gods of the plant planets,"
prays the Hippy,
"May you send us straight to heaven upon the day we
pass out dead from the ganja. Amen."

"Amen," responds the congregation of two.

"Will you marry me?" she asks the hidden turtle.
"Really?" he's taken the spiritual bait.
"If you take it with one breath,"
she sighs,
"I will suck you off, forever."

"Okay smoke that shit," Peacock breaks the silence. She thought it, he heard it in his head, she thought those words, and he will show her how much of a pothead he can...and the Hippy plummets the jug into the tub water. Peacock ignites the lighter— Jimi's "Wait Until Tomorrow," rolls into the soundscape— She waves the flame over the grass as the Hippy gently raises the jug. A tornado of smoke spirals into the empty space of the jug. The vacuum is strong. All the smoke of the bowl is sucked inward. Nothing leaks until she removes the lighter and the Hippy fights the vacuum from releasing the cap as smoke pushes its way out through the wire screen in the metal bowl— "Go!" she yells, but first he's gotta twist the cap off and then he dive-bombs his lips around the mouth of the jug. Peacock puts a hand on his head and pushes him faster. He sucks it in. All too much. He reflexes back. Smoke escapes everywhere. How much did he get in? And he's on his back. Flat on the tiles. His eyes are going to pop if doesn't keep them shut. He exhales half of the jug's smoke into the room. There is no visibility. The Hippy is cold stoned. His body jerks. Silence. He gasps and immediately begins to cough. And cough. Coughing. Coughing. Gag. Cough. Puke a little. Gag. Spit. Cough. Gotta cough it out. Cough. Clear the throat. Cough. Try to gag. Drool. Wipe the chin. "Fuck man. That hits hard," and he curls himself into a ball in the corner by the door. "Hit it Peacock," he suggests. "Fuck yeah," and she turns, hands the Bald One the lighter, and swipes the cap from the edge of the bath. "Hand me that bud," she asks the Bald One. He breaks it up a bit and taps it into the bowl. "Alright that's good. But dude, don't put the flame on the weed," she tells him. "Yeah, I know," he says. "Do you? Do you know?" she questions him. "Yes. Now come on!" he's frustrated. "Awe. Still want to kiss me huh?"—

"Come on. Just do it," he says.

She smiles and goes for it pushing the jug down as he waves the flame just above the bowl as she gently submerges the gravity bong and then she takes the entire jug as one of the Chinese Brothers had drunk the sea. The Bald One is impressed, *"I guess she doesn't need me."* The Peacock gently straightens her back into a meditative state as she calmly holds the entire jug of puff in her lungs. Streams of smoke rise from her nostrils and she eases the rest out of her partially open lips. Her rainbow toe nails curl into the bathroom rug of white yarn and the Peacock spreads her magnificent tail and allows her hidden wings to burst from her Stoned Jesus print shirt. Her oversized skirt hides her monstrous rainbow scaled dragon feet. She fills the room. The psychedelic feathers wave in the smoke and when the Bald One reaches out to kiss her dark purple feathered belly she shrinks, and flies away through a crack in the bathroom window. And the Bald One asks the Hippy, "Was that girl for real?"

"Totally."

#13

an

URG

ENCY

in   the   night.

There was a sense of urgency to the night. Last night. Now it was morning. The mornings were darker than the nights to Collins. The spiked hands of the timepiece on the wall spun diamonds into his eyes. Collins couldn't open his front door. His grip was slippery when wet— even more moist and humid after his older brother, Michael, went on a misunderstood rant spitting in Collins' face about cold cuts and sour pickles. Collins was soaked to the bone; milk toast to his own uncertainty. A door is not like the pores of the human's skin. If they were, Collins would have easily seeped through the wood to the outside world once again. He would have been part of the community.

*

The first sound came from the closet. A thump. Something must have fallen, but Collins had left that room empty. Collins did not believe in closets. Collins believed that if a door was attached to hinges then there was an actual room on the other side. Sliding doors did not count. French doors do. This closet had a doorknob. He kept that room empty. Nothing could have fallen. There was no sound. The room was empty. Ignore it. It did not happen. A ricochet of sound. That's what it was. From outside. Maybe just his heart? It was beating particularly fast this evening, this morning.

He has been tense lately.

Collins ignored the thump and began his business restocking the columns of newspapers that cut narrow halls through his three-bedroom apartment, second floor, partial high-rise, not off the park, off the alley. He hated heights, but hated the first floor even more. He despised the laughter of the park and preferred the moans of homeless sleeping throughout the day. Somehow a few of the newspaper columns had tumbled over and spread loose pages along the floor. Did that happen yesterday?

The days have started to melt into one another. Mother had left the apartment to him in her passing. That's what he remembered anyhow. He's still a little fuzzy about that.

The thump had come from the closet where Mother hung their school jackets when they were young. Michael would always push his way in first. He was older. Stronger. This had led Michael to believe that the harder he was on his baby brother; the stronger Collins would become. Instead, Collins was repressing a deep harrowing vengeance in his stomach. That gut rage of knots hasn't changed since Mother's passing; in fact, it has grown substantially like a cancer on the soul. But then again, all of that is still a little fuzzy and he has never been diagnosed with cancer. He did have his tonsils removed.

He stopped talking back then. Mother had claimed they botched the operation, sued, lost, but Collins still would not speak, that was until he had something to finally say.

"Mother's in the mattress," he would joke to himself with each newspaper he restocked— School shootings, child rapists, broken borders —"Mother's in the mattress," and then he'd giggle. THUD! Another sound. This one from the kitchen, but he hasn't cooked in weeks, probably months. Collins rarely used absolutes when thinking about time. The nights have begun to melt together as well. Didn't matter. A second sound is a sound to be alarmed about. Maybe it was his girlfriend, but he didn't have a girlfriend, did he? The dog? No, he died about eighteen years ago. Maybe it was Michael? Maybe Michael never really left? Collins had no choice. He had to go to the sound. He forced himself to creep— carefully —to his cooking quarters which had a three paneled, paint chipped swinging door— A door his sweaty palms could potentially open because there was no knob to slip up on. He stabbed the center of his palm with the needle he kept pinned to his shirt. He used this metal tool to help wake him up from the dream he thought he was constantly trapped in. He bled. He wasn't dreaming. Fuck. He's never dreaming. Ever.

There was nothing on the other side of this kitchen door. Collins was sure of that. Was he sure of that? What he wasn't sure of was how horrifying the nothing could be. Would it be the oven silently leaking gas into his home? Maybe an electrical fire behind the busted refrigerator? Couldn't be the rotting fingers in the cupboard tapping against the cereal boxes to be set free

— They can't move? —

And the nothing scraped along the inside of Collins' skin, and he knew fear. Fear. Anxiety. Baby diapers and shoe polish.

!CRACK!

This time below him; under the splintered hardwood planks. "To the sea with you," whispered his brother into his kindergarten ears before submerging Collins into the full bath of scalding water. He couldn't breathe. Never held his breath before. Collins hadn't ever even swum in a pool before— let alone an ocean —he opened his mouth to scream silently underwater and swallowed. Bath water, swirled in soap scum, bubbles, dirt, grime, and blood that had spilt from his own nostrils all vacuumed up into his small child lungs and Michael pulled his baby brother from the bath, laughing. Collins was rushed to the hospital by the neighbor. "He slipped," said Michael. Collins nodded, agreed.

*

Collins let the kitchen door close back into place. Gently. Don't startle the sounds. Gently Collins. Close it slow. He was not going in there. He wasn't going anywhere. He was going to wait for another sound before he let his guard down. Something, someone, was in here with him— Somewhere. Maybe he left the window open last night? Michael had him in such a stir after flushing his medication down the toilet, that he may have opened the window to cool down? He wouldn't. That would be insane. Collins had been suicidal before, but an open window, he would have had to be fully out of his skull to do that. He wasn't crazy. He had gone crazy before— In 7th grade —Michael put Acid in his sandwich. Collins never forgot those twisted 72 hours. It was a Wednesday. Collins was already a recluse by junior high school. He sat alone at the far end of the cafeteria beside the trashcan. At the least he got a little human contact when the kids would come by to scrape their leftovers into the dumpster. Mom made salami on white. He felt something odd in his mouth. Something from the sandwich was not breaking up. He bit and ground with his molars, but to no end. He remembered salivating on his new button up Mom had bought him at the department store. Collins used his tongue to find the sticky pieces against his gums and used his grubby fingers to peel them off. Paper? Two small squares and twenty minutes later all hell broke loose burning fires of dismembering youth into his pupils. He saw into everyone and everything. He saw the blood and felt the inside of all of their flesh. Flesh that smothered him into a cocoon of fluid that ate its way through his own skin like the acid he had ingested. The counselor's never blamed Collins' oddness on the bad trip. They contributed his delusions on a predisposition from his father's side— His father hanged himself in the coat room when the boys were barely in preschool. Collin's found his father's blue, bloated, naked body hung and swaying over the feces that had dropped upon the death. Michael pushed Collins inside with Dad. Michael locked the door to the room.

!RIP!

Another sound. A different sound— Rip, rip, Snap, snap, Crank —He batted his head left— look —then right, listen.

There is a lunatic tearing fabric in here, in this apartment, Mother's apartment. Scratch. It's an uneven scratch that gets caught up on its self. Collins buried his face into his palms. Pressed his eyes deeper into his skull. Must focus on where it's coming from. Listen Collins— For G-d's sake listen for once. Crank. Crank. Something metal revolved on itself. Metal scrapping and tangled against rusted springs. The sounds of fucking from the bedroom. This is too much. Is Dad having sex with Mother, again? Why do they leave the door open? Michael's got another girl in there, doesn't he? No, Michael's gone…but the fucking…it's too loud…sounds so violent— Collins closed himself in the coat room to get away.

He thought it had been long enough. It had been two, possibly three hours since he heard a sound from outside this room, this closet. He felt close to his father's absence. Protected. But it was time to be a man again. You have to go out there. Not all the way, but you can't stay here. Remember what happens to people when they stay in in this room. They turn blue. They fill with air and water. They shit themselves. Then they take you. They zip you up in a black plastic bag. They take you to the morgue. Your family will have to identify you. Then they burn you Collins. They burn your flesh off and set your ashes on the TV because that's where dead people go. That's where dead people go Collins, dead people. On TV. Broken TVs that never play shows.

*

That's where dead people go. That's where dead people go to
die. That's for dead people. Big blue bloated dead people
Collins. Dead. People.

*

Collins burst from the door. He tripped over his own feet. The
tumble sent his malnourished skeleton of a figure into a tower
of newspapers. They shuffled everywhere. He scrambled to
his feet. Used the stack of papers to keep his balance. This
column fell as well. His socked feet scattered the loose pages.
He turned back towards the coat room. The door was wide
open. The inside — dark, empty. Empty. A void. Empty.

Father had been taken away.
Father was on the TV,
dead.

*

He could only imagine what it felt like to suffocate to death.
He could only fathom a knife in his back from his brother.

That fucking brother of his.

That brother that locked him in the coat room with Dad—

That fucking brother that took him to a hooker.
A hooker with warts. A hooker with warts and gonorrhea.
When he was eighteen. When he was drunk. When he was...

"You're a retard,"
Michael stacked the deck into Collins drunk, mentally
disturbed, adolescence in an eighteen-year old's
skin and bones; blood beat and all.

"This is the only way you'll get laid," the older brother said in biblical terms to his burden of nothing. Collins meant nothing to Michael. Collins was Michael's ego. Michael had confused his conscious with his ego. His Id was on strike and Michael had less going on upstairs than a dumb version of his baby brother. Michael pushed Collins through the graffiti door, in the back-alley; their local prostitute shop.

Collins had to take a month's dose of antibiotics. Puss. Puke. Sickness. Fear. Puke and Vomit. All the same. It's all just the same. Everyone is a disease.

*

That fucking brother that…SNAP! Something's snapped. Snap. Again. Came from the bedroom. That's where that one came from; this Collins knew for sure. One foot at a time like the therapists taught him. Slowly sliding his socks along the hardwood floor. Wouldn't want to make a sound. Wears socks to prevent splinters. If the bedroom hears his footsteps, it's all over; he'll never catch the culprit.

Sweat poured from his hair. He could taste the salt on his lips. One foot at a time. Slide. Slide. The bedroom door was firmly closed. When had he closed it? Remember Collins— Did you or didn't you close the door?

"I can't remember," he said aloud then shushed his self, whispering, "Shut up, you numbskull. You're going to get us both punished."

Both? Who was he talking too? Wait. Who's talking to me? So much sound, but he's alone. He is always alone. Not even a dog or a rat. Probably just roaches. Yeah, roaches. Bedbugs and roaches. That's what spoke to him…scratch that…that's what sounds like snapping popcorn behind that bedroom door. He had to open it. No time to hesitate. They might escape. They might just scatter and come back tomorrow. If they come back tomorrow then they'll be back in week, then a month— Won't leave him alone for years. He couldn't handle that much company. One's enough. He, himself, and I. The arm had begun to itch. The sweat had created a heat rash. Last time he broke out in a rash that fucking brother of his had taught him how to use an iron. "Here. This will make you forget about the itches," Michael said as he had placed the scalding hot iron on Collins prepubescent shoulder.

*

After the bedroom door—

After the door, he'll tend to the iron and itches.
After the bedroom door—

Life will get back to normal.

Peace will prevail.

After this door
…and the knob turned in his sweaty palm and he opened it, slowly. Opened to the dimly lit room; light crept in from aged holes in the window shade. Two twin beds press up against each other, held together by a set of sweaty sheets pulled tight. The pillowcases stained with grease and the windows are consistently fogged from the moisture trapped within. The mold has blotched and spotted the inside of the glass and the sent is no better off with incense. The wallpaper peals, yet Collins saw no bugs scurry upon his entrance. He had a sudden sense of calm—

A calm that rushed upon him like that of a lightning storm from the eye of a hurricane. A calm so bombastic it was completely silent. The nerves under his mind sparked out of control. His neck was irritatingly numbed from the pain.

The tearing tightness along his spine pulled open his rib cage. His heartbeat was not thumping. He could not feel his heart. Who could care about any of that when things were so loud they were quiet. When things are were...

—CRACK!   STAB! FUMBLE AND TUMBLE! BEAT! BEAT! BEAT! CHOKE HIM! CHOKE THAT MUTHER FUCKER! CHOKE AND GAG! GAG ON THAT SHIT YOU FUCK FACE PILE OF DOG FUCK! SQUEEZE THAT NECK! TIGHTER! HE'S STILL PANTING! SHUT UP! SHUT UP, MIKE! RIP! TEAR! FLESH! FLESH RIGHT OFF THE BONE! FUCK YOU! YOU DON'T OWN ME! CUT HIS FINGERS OFF! SCRAMBLE! TRAMBLE! KICK! GOT ONE! THE INDEX! SUCKER! KICK HIM! IN THE BALLS! STEP ON HIS BALLS! STEP! USE YOUR HEEL! YES! YES! BREAK THOSE BALLS! BREAK EM! STOP MOVING! DIE ALREADY YOU FUCK! DIE!—

...and then there was a real knock at the door. Collins whipped his head around to look out the doorway of the bedroom. His mind said no more. He stared at the front door in utter fear. That sound was real.

"Who is it?" Collins asked.

He should have cut his own vocal chords out last night.
Yeah, that was the biggest mistake. Talking to the walls was useless and going out in public was disgusting.

Germs everywhere.

Antibiotics.
Puss. Gag. Vomit.

It was all the same.
Everyone is a disease. That would have kept him quiet.

No more vocal chords.
Maybe tomorrow.
Then another knock at
the door. Two knocks
to be exact. He
counted them. Knock,
"One." Knock, "Two."

They must not
have heard his
request.
He had asked
nicely enough.
They wouldn't
ignore him,
now would
they?
But then
again—

Tomorrow he'll use
Father's old pliers to
rip out his larynx.
Collins had been
ignored before.
Father didn't say shit
when he was hanging
in the closet by his
neck. Father wouldn't
even help him open
the door.

Dad just hung there like a bloated whale...

...with his dick shriveled up into his abdomen.

KNOCK—KNOCK!

*

"Who is it?" Collins asked, this round he speaks with more conviction; pride in his home, his inherited home. Home sweet home, "I do not accept solicitation of any sort."

"Collins, it's Susan. Your neighbor?"

Collin's took a moment to consider this real human sound.

"Not the ZCA?" Collins questions this woman from the safety of the door.

"Susan. Sue, Zan."

> "That's a woman's voice from the hallway. The long room on the outside of the apartment door. The hallway that has even more doors. More rooms. Rooms within rooms. The same hallway that leads to the stairs and the elevator, those are not rooms, Collins is no fool," he thought to himself, aloud through the peephole, "The same stairs and elevator that lead to the first floor—The first floor that leads through the lobby to the glass doors that lead to the street. The street where people ooze with disease. I can see her fattened face through the peephole; she is beautiful, friendly, Susan my neighbor."

Susan's a pasty faced, black haired, blood red lipstick vampire that has been kind to him in the past. She has never bothered him during the day before. Susan usually checks on Collins after dark. What time is it? It is dark outside. The day is over. Maybe the sounds will finally stop. Maybe Collins won't have to kill her after all. Collins couldn't kill Susan. Collins couldn't hurt a fly. "Eat it!" Michael pressed the jar of insects into Collins teeth, "EAT IT!"

*

"Happy Halloween," Susan called from behind the door. She held up a single cupcake with orange frosting, a pumpkin decorated toothpick lodged in its head, and cherry blood syrup that curled out from the puncture, "I brought you something. Open up."

*

Susan was patient. It always took Collins three to five minutes to gather the nerve to open his front door. "What is it?" he asked, sweat dribbling from his matted hair; the remaining strands of hair that he hadn't pulled out, as of yet.

————————————————click—

"It'll keep things quieter for you tonight, Collins," Susan said as she gently placed the cupcake into his palm, "It's Halloween. You know how loud it gets on Halloween."
"Very loud."
"Yes, very loud. Look, just eat it. It's Pot Pumpkin."
"I don't use medications."
"Relax; it's recreational now. Just eat it, sit back, eat it, watch some TV."

> *But that's where you go when you die.*
> *Collins was nervous again. The TV?*
> *Maybe Collins would do something else.*

"Is it poisonous?"
"No baby. It's marijuana. Trust me, you'll feel better."
"I'm okay. Thank you?" he said looking down at the dessert in his palm. He thought about stabbing his other palm with the needle, but then she wouldn't leave. Wait until she leaves. Then you can decide if you want out of the dream or not.

"You get some rest. I'm going out. I won't be around until the morning— I can't check up on you tonight per usual," she steps closer, but not into the doorframe, kisses his check, but not really, "Eat it. You'll feel better."

*

"Tomorrow?"

*

"Say hello to Michael and Mother for me."
"Ok."

*   *

*

"Happy Halloween, sweetie."

*

*

Collins closed the door, locked

all three deadbolts,

and

strung

the

chain.

*

Maybe I should make some soup?

Collins looked at the cupcake in his hand. You better do what she said. Yes Collins, that's the best idea. Eat the cupcake. Marijuana? What is it? I thought you smoke marijuana. Try a bite. She said it is good for you. Collins took a small bite, a nibble. It's good. Pumpkin. A strange bitter taste too it.

Herbal. He licked the icing from his upper lip. Sugar. No real taste to the sugary dyed orange cream. He took another bite. Bigger than the first. Then another. And another. Two more until he completed the trick or treat and went to the window that he was sure he had mistakenly cracked open, but no it was safely locked tight *(pause, breath, it's just glass)* Outside on the streets he followed the ghosts and goblins with his twitchy eyes. Creeps and Killers scattered around cars and approached doorsteps. He heard nothing. The cupcake had already begun to work.

Collins; deep breath *(pause, breathe, it's just Halloween)* Stoned. Bread. See.

The breath stayed inside this time. No more panting. Take another breath Collins. Ah, relief in the chest. The ribs have slid back into place. Your eyes are heavy. Maybe it's time for bed. You're plenty tired, Collins. Go to sleep. Lay down and drift away. No more lies tonight. No one is in here. You are safe. No more lies tonight. Just go to the bedroom and relax.

He grabbed the lump of a comforter from the blood stained, brown carpet of the bedroom and draped it along the two twin beds. Collins crawled in. Covered his head. Cried. Felt better. Laughed. Cried about laughing. Heard nothing. The cupcake is doing the trick. Or treat? He really did feel calm and relaxed. The lumpy mattresses were barely moving under him tonight. The tearing of the two sets of human fingernails from inside the beds were highly muted. The reminder of sound was the memory of rusted springs pressed against the open skulls of Mother and Michael when they were fighting to get free from inside the mattresses—and the gurgling of their lungs, filled with fluid and phlegm, sound less like a death rattle now that he's stoned. I believe Collins will get a good night's rest this Halloween. And tomorrow? November first? Well tomorrow, if it gets too bad again, the sounds don't stop, the complaining of a body starved for weeks, well then, time to learn how to sleep alone. Sell it on the web; used mattress, full of meat, stained, free. Then they'll come and take Michael and Mother away. They'll burn their flesh and put them on the TV with Dad. Tomorrow. November first. "Goodnight Mom. Fuck you Michael."

And Collins fell fast asleep into a real dream.

The End.

#14

TOP SELF

Stop light. "Come on." Tap, tap on steering wheel. Turns up radio. A commercial. "New tires, who needs 'em. Fix it with Flix," Keeve says in unison with the narrator, "Flix the fix. Come on! Oh green," and he rolls through the intersection making the first immediate right into the driveway of the spot. "Fix it with Flix," and he pulls in between two Range Rovers, army green & candy red. Keeve drives a Ford F-100, matte-black, tinted windows, with a rusted bumper. Hops out, leaves his wallet in the car, approaches the glass doors, pats his ass, no wallet, struts back to the cab, pops the door, pops the glove compartment, grabs his leather, flips through the dollars, $350, "cool, cool," and heads on into the spot.

Nod to the security guard, big in blue, hefty, dark aviators, says he, "don't like the mirrors 'cause I don't like people lookin' at themselves." Keeve couldn't agree more. Guard nods back, Keeve steps up to the window. ID and Medical Card. She's an attractive one. Red hair, dark skin, loops, plump lips, Keeve peaks over the rail a tad, doesn't want to be rude, but she is attractive. Can't see her figure. "Returning?"
"Yeah."
"Ok," and she writes his name out onto the ledger.

*

She lifts her head. Looks at Keeve with her brown eyes, "Here you go," hands him his cards back, "It'll be just a sec." Keeve takes the cards, "Thanks," and sits on one of the white leather stools. Guard nods at Keeve again, Keeve nods back. Hip Hop is fills the waiting area while fun facts about THC play on the HD screen attached to the wall. "Busy?"
"No."
"Slow?"
"Kinda."
"Cool."
The guard nods, removes his glasses, cleans the lenses, checks out the girl, looks back at Keeve, smiles, Keeve nods. "You can go back now," she says leaning out the window. She's got to be cute all over, just has to be. Keeve is a believer. He makes his way to the door, she buzzes him into the weed room.

*

The waft of weed is always high as you enter the weed room...today it was slightly less waft-y.
"Afternoon," says the beautiful budtender girl behind the counter.
"What's up," Keeve plays it cool. He's seen her before, 10, 20 times before.
"What can we get you today?" she asks.
"Um," Keeve looks around the spot, so many vapes, so many alternative options, where's the weed, the flower, the real stuff, "What gives? You don't have flower today?"

"Real low," she steps out of the way revealing two large nearly empty jars on the top shelf behind her, "All we got left is Spiderwillow and some super potent mix shake."

"Mix shake? That like house weed?"

"No, it's what we call the Top Shelf Salad," she shakes the jar, "Leftovers from the bottom of all the top shelf jars."

"That kinda sounds delicious," Keeve says squinting his eyes at the jar. She grabs it, unscrews the top, leans it towards Keeve's nose. She has immaculate emerald eyes, accentuated in glow from her dark black skin. K smells the contents of the jar, "You could bottle that smell and sell that," he tells her, she laughs, "Yeah, I guess you could," and she screws the wide top back on and places it on the counter, "You want some of that?"

"Top Shelf Salad? Not sure," Keeve needs to think about it. What's to think about Keeve, you only got two choices. That's the problem, he's only got two choices. What kind of America is it with only two choices of weed? We legalized this stuff for a reason and now it's late September and you only got two choices, "Is the Spiderwillow any good?"

"All top shelf," she grabs the Spiderwillow jar, unscrews it, puts it right up to Keeve's nose, "Smell it. A hybrid."

*

Let's get real here,
Keeve does not care about smelling weed
he cares about smoking weed
he cares about stocking himself
and his pal
up with some dank weed
to keep them high for the next week.
He doesn't want to come back here in a couple days
just because he smoked it all.
He'd come back to get a date with this Budtender,
but he's not asking,
he's asking for a week's supply
of getting high.

*

"Strong, huh?" she asks, "3.5 grams for $80," re-screws the

top back on and places it beside the salad.

"Wow, uh, you got any bottom shelf?" he asks, definitely disqualifying himself for a date anytime in the near future.

"Yeah, no, it's really slow this month."

"Why?"

"I don't know."

"Man, I really needed bulk," he scratches his head.

"You gotta ration it out. Don't roll joints with this, this stuff is made for a bong...or a pipe."

"So, no bottom shelf."

"Nope."

"Middle shelf?"

"I don't think that's a term."

Pause.

She waits.

He thinks.

She waits.

He wants bottoms shelf.

She waits.

He thinks.

He wants her.

She waits.

He thinks.

"So, no basic weed, just this high-grade shit?"

"Yup."

"Hm."

?

"you're cute, if you get some salad I'll smoke it with you"

"are you kidding"

"no, baby"

?

Hmmm.

"Let me see how much I got," he says aloud pulling out his

wallet. She waits. He pries it open, flips through the bills in their pouch...three fifty...oh yeah, he remembers, "I got three hundred fifty." She is impressed, that was not what she was expecting.

"Oh, you'll be set dude, you'll buy us all out, but you'll be set."

"I smoke a lot of weed."

"I hear that," she says, "So, which do you want?"

"A date."

"Excuse me?"

"Well, if I'm buying you all out, does it matter?"

"Did you just ask me out?"

"Uh, accidentally?"

"Cute. Yer very cute. So, yeah, I guess yer right, all of it...if it adds up," and she begins her process as Keeves keeps his eyes on her two-tone shades of purple fingernails. Watch her hands, don't look at her, don't creep her out...why did you ask her out? She's totally forgetting it happened. She's probably got a boyfriend, or three. They'd kill him for asking her out. Beat him silly in the least. She places the green plastic pill bottle on the scale, resets the scale, funnels the contents of the Mixed Salad into the bottle. "Bye bye salad," she says, he chuckles, she screws the cap back on, clink, and places it's empty self on the shelf, turns back around, unscrews the Spiderwillow, zzzzshoop-clink, grabs another bottle, puts it on the scale, restarts the scale, grabs the elongated tweezers, and begins to pick bud after bud, dropping them into the pill bottle, as the scale numbers creep up then balance out, creep up, then balance out, creep up...

"What are you doing that you need so much weed this week?

"Stuff."

"Like work? or Play?"

"A little of both, I guess."

"What kinda stuff?"

*

First, I'd take us to the lake.
No, no smoking until we get there.
Don't want to ruin our initial high of the day.

Spend that high on the beautiful lake.
I'll make sure it's warm out. Hot even. Have to swim.
Let's get high.
You said this stuff is for bongs and pipes,
I rolled us a blunt.
Yeah, that's right, just for us.
You can handle it.
I've seen the way you manage that counter.
You're the weed princess, the princess of weed
the daughter of the weed king
the lover of the weed prince
We'll shotgun the whole blunt until our lips meet
and we'll strip naked
swim in the lake
love in the

*

"Stuff, ya know?"

"Totally."

"You got any plans this week?"

"My girlfriends are all going to the waterpark."

"Really? I was just talking with my boy about that place."

"I prefer nature, ya? I don't want my ass rubbing down no plastic tube in pee water."

"Deer pee in the river."

"I guess you're right, but like, that shit flows out to the ocean, so that's okay," and she drops the last bud of the shop into his bottle, "Op, that's it...you came up short, let me add that up."

Pause.
She calculates.
He waits.
She calculates.
He waits.
So, attractive.
She calculates.
So, sexy.
He waits.
Funny.

She calculates.
Sweet.
He waits.
Rich?
She calculated.

The cash register prints out the receipt, "Three Twenty-Five." He pulls the cash from his wallet, counts out $325, hands her the bills. "Where you gonna take me with your twenty-five bucks?" she says, CLING, the cash register drawer opens, CLUNK, she flips up the dollar tabs, put the proper bills in their proper beds, closes the drawer with her hip, rips the receipt, staples it to the paper bag containing his two bottles, hands it to him, "Thanks," he says, tips her a 5 'cause he has no ones and leaves, completely missing her acceptance to a date...reaches his car...realizes his mistake...never returns to that spot, forever more.

Don't be like Keeve.

#15
CREATI
VE kUSH

. Creativity comes in seven sizes :.

　　　　. Fat . Skinny . Chubby . Lumpy . Skeletal . Flabby .
. Kush .

. Creativity is easy to comprehend :.

. Smart . Stupid . Gullible . Conniving . Claustrophobic.
. Egocentric .

. Creativity warrants investigation :.

. Camouflage . Neanderthal. Hollywood . Alabama .
. Texas Rangers .

. Creativity is a puppy :.

. Lick . Love . Mouth . Love . Attention . Need . Drool .
. Shit .

. Creativity derives from patience :.

. Dry . Sand . Melt . Compress . Matrimony . Clientele .
. Sex .

. Creativity is undebatable :.

. Dictatorship . Inventor . Idea . Design . Writer . Trend.

. Empathy .

. Creativity consults liars, thieves, villains, crooks, & angels :.

. Lawyers . Lawmakers . Lunatics . Leaches . Lions .
. Leprechauns .

>kUSHalone< CreativekUsh

kUsh canna-instoppable
prideful
greenalicious
delight
afternoonmorningeveningnightmorningnoonafternoonevenin
g
n
i
g
h
t
?
thepresidentyellsandyellsandcriesandweepsandratsandcatswi
t
h
o
u
t
ourKuSH
Flauntitorfightit
itstitsnasswithcocksntwats
.

stalling, the inedible, sleep...

#16

foggy
FUTURES

London had become an utter bore. He started dabbing between dabbing. Burn after burn. He didn't mind so much. He didn't mind anything these days. The rains were misting the sidewalks. He dabbed some more. The reflection of the city in the puddles of fog would get even clearer through the glaze along his eyes.

Every couple of days the girl from the thrift shop would stop by and do a dab or two. They thought about fucking, but London had just become such a bore. She'd stand naked in her mind blindly staring at the wet cobblestones. Her dream was full frontal in the thrift store window. She would sway her planked hips ever so slightly. You could barely notice unless you were beside her. She was lovely. The men would collect along the sidewalk. Was she real or a manikin? Robotics? No, those were banned a half a century ago. She was real. Or not. The men didn't care, they were attracted either way; why else would they ban such a productive sect of society? So, she swayed, they gathered, their wives will never buy a thing. They would elbow each other showing face to their neighbor saying, "I think she likes me. She keeps looking into my eyes."— The mist against the thrift store window had begun to drip. Water balls cutting lines in the clean glass. Faceless bodies walk on by, but no one steps inside these days and instead of dreaming she ate edibles for breakfast and folded torn jeans in the backroom, she swayed naked, and swayed some more. No one buys torn jeans since London had become such an unbearable bore.

Every couple of days he'd put a thick coat over his flannel and walk a mile or so to the Queen's castle, but she wouldn't see him because she couldn't bear to go outside herself since London had become such a bore. She blamed it on the misfits who had all gone to New York and the flux between the Hip-Hop Party and House Majority. These broken iconographic images behind his eyes didn't deter him from waiting patiently at the gates watching the red guards pace in honor of the bore called London. The Americas had become too organized, retracted, open, common, and seductive for him to live there anymore. Paradise Manor, the new capital, central to all things beautiful, better than a wall, more appealing and powerful than the canal, this was the bridge between the war, this was where peace was made, where demanding systems systematically united on the backs of the Americas' citizens. All were now the color of the earth, all were one, no North, no South, No Center, all Green, all Weed Party. Tempting, draining, paradise. They never allowed Robotics. They were determined to keep of the flesh, genetics, new-mans. It was the only way to stop the re-exodus back to the Englands. First came the wealthiest. They were easily able to afford all the Robotic Sexuals...but then the boredom struck the rest of the people and that's when the middle class lost their men. Good to be a poor American for once. Anyhow, he stayed in London because everyone loved the way his friend swayed in the window. He'd gotten in the habit of vape hits when the nutcrackers turned their backs. After, he generally got a pastry and a pack of smokes that he'd distribute to the poor who suffered the most from this grey town by the sea being such a sudden never-ending bore. London never changed, just expanded for real this time. Americas and Englands. It was a fine world with only two borders.

No one visited the desolate plains of other abandoned lands.
She dreamed one day she would.
He promised they would both go there to die,
and that would make use of the past.

They would meet sometimes on Saturdays. That's when they could watch the bombs bursting in the distant islands. He felt it was all so very fickle to un-name the continents. The Kings with their pockets so full of gold had nothing more to do these days than avoid the conflict and emasculate the populated worlds into small withered islands that once were Somalia, Syria, Granada, Los Angeles, Cambridge, and the likes now known as tourist traps with surf shops and spiritual accountants serving only the taxman himself who serves the King and the Queens. And London never got excited and never was there a rebellion in years. This is what was considered the bore.

Saturday was their day to smoke the joints instead. Only Saturday— Their day to awaken the ocean's child. The boy who stood two hundred feet over his mother's washing tides. The boy who would lift his evaporating hands away from his eyes and press them into the clouds that were his father. The clouds would shape shift to the Londoner's every whim and will. Some were that of a Capricorn, and the others a school of fish, with six more the shapes of blossoming flowers illuminated by the fires of the burning human sacrifice with smoke billowing from their stove tops, up and out of London's chimneys. By five she would always yawn and remind them both how London became such a bore.

#17
CAT fights

The two distinctly different colored Desert Kats liked leaning against the chain-link at sundown. They were discarded Barbies at birth. One was lean and short with barn red hair. The other, leaner, a foot taller, bleached blonde, silver in the sun. She could have been a model if she was born west of the desert. They pay good enough for San Bernardino nudes. Desert nudes just be artsy-tartsy, or crackhead amateurs. And no matter what they coulda been, if born different, they were here then, here now, and maybe cross town tomorrow. "We two like to scatter to the intake and that take is everything that sounds fun." That's who they were. Do you know who you are?

Both skanks wandered the long strip mall avenue of dollar stores, fast food, gas stops, and $30 motels closed down for various reasons while the town renovates at the speed of a snail. "Carmalita ain't no worthness," Kim gossips as she picks at her torn blue nylon. Sienna the coulda-been, woulda-been, busty, chemically bulimic waistline says through her ten-hour gum as she adjusts her white leather nine-inch heel, "Yea, she a pillow case. We gonna get some weed?" A car passes. They didn't know that one. Better. Neither of these two are ready to slut out quite yet. Whore is to be exact— If they fuck. Sometimes they try to cut before the fuck. That's being a slut. Kind of. More a of cunt. Either way, not a whore.

"Jesse got some."

"When Jesse coming?"

"Jesse ain't coming."

"So why we get from him?"

"We ain't getting from Jesse. We gonna go Hensey Blvd meet Dylan."

"Dylan only holdin' yella dust."

"You fuck Fanny three weeks 'go?"

"Nah I got too drunk. I puked on her ass," they giggle.

A car pulls to the side of the curb. Sienna knows him. Jeff. Jeff'll be nice to her if he's in the right mood. Gave her a $50 for just talking at Carl's Jr one time. A black eye when she asked for a stay after rimming him for tying her off. "I need a favor," he says through his passenger window. "Alright. What favor?" Sienna's willing to listen. She knows Kim really wants to listen. Kim leans into the window beside Sienna. Sienna's playing with Jeff's fingertips as he tries to explain, "I left my room key at some place."

"Yea. So, what of it sweetie?"

"I need a few," he's tweaking, "I need some cash."

"You asking us for money?"

"Has to be like secret. No one can know," he says as he eyeballs his glove compartment, "I'll make it up to you."

"How you gonna make it up to us? You gonna blow us?"

"Yeah, if that's what you want, anything."

"You're a real nut-job. My pussy don't do favors."

"Well, we know," Kim interjects.

"That ain't gonna help," Sienna hisses back at her curb-mate.

"Go fuck yourself, bitch. I do it for you Jeffy," Kim is trying to swipe Sienna's off and on.

"No. Gotta be you," he says right to Sienna.

"You smell of loyalty. No one gonna fuck you right if you feel like you're gonna stick around."

"Only Sienna."

"Move on fool," she says as she shoe-flies the piece of shit away, takes a step back onto the curb, then another, and another, leans back against the chain link, it wavers from starved weight of this silver haired Desert Kitten, and lights her cigarette she's slid from her ear, "This place sucks so bad," and chips away at her fingernail paint. Kim leans deeper into the car window, "You got any weed?" she asks Jeff. He can't deal with this and drives off. "Cock sucker!" flips him the bird. The car disappears into the blue side of the sunset towards the lightless shadowed darkness of their trash decorated desert town on the forgotten side of the two-lane 10 freeway stretching from the shores of LaLa land. The desert was closer to Vegas. The desert wins for rationality...so say the Desert Rats of East California and the Porcupines in Texas.

"Carmalita used to hook up the smoke," Sienna reminds Kim picking gum off her skirt.

"Shit dirty. Fuck Carmalita."

"She had good smoke though."

"Carmalita's a coward."

"She ain't coming back."

"That what I say. Bitch scared o' me."

"You kill that stray shat."

"I cut her. I cut her right in the cootchie," sexy Sienna says slicing the air with her broken fingernails. K turns to the road and pussy flashes the oncoming car, "I gotta pee," but she won't, not here, maybe down the block, not behind a bush, prickly the desert can be— is, "Where we getting the weed?"

"Billy-Sue. She doing cleaning at a Four Room. Stays there too. Trailer in the back."

"Billy-Sue got weed?"

"She got a joint or something."

The high-heels are a bitch to walk in this early in the night. The fucking sun dive bombs behind those surrounding mountains like hours earlier than the shore towns.

"I ain't walking in these. We gotta wait for a ride."

"Who we waiting for?"

"You got one of those pay cards?"

"Gift cards. Target and stuff."

"Where you get them?"

"That john had a purse full of them. I got 'em when he passed out."

"Was he drunk?"

"I was drunk. He was a thief though. I thieved him back."

"Solid."

"Just walk barefoot."

"Yeah I guess. You got a card on you now?"

"Nah, left 'em."

"Where you stayin?"

"Ya know."

"How long now?"

"Couple weeks. But they asked me to go somewhere. But I was all like, where I gonna go, ya know?"

"Why they ask you that?"

"Right?"

"This place is all assholes."

"I never used their dishes and shit. They say I gotta clean too. Why I gotta clean? I ain't live there. My name not on the lease and shit."

"They treat you like you gotta pay like a hotel, right? What they act all rich n' shit?"

"Nah she got a baby coming. He ain't the Daddy."

"How long you be there now?"

"Month or so. Why you so curious?"

"You fuck the Daddy yet?"

"I said he ain't the Daddy. And no. Not yet. Shit's fucked up, yo. If he got a ugly down there, then I gotta move, ya know? Ain't the Four Room on Stocktons?"

"No. Stocktons down two blocks. Four Room's off Bouton. Past the tennis courts."

"Mama played tennis when I was little. She fucked a country club dude and we used to go too, ya know?"

"I hope she's got a bowl."

"She got blunts or something. Think she's banging a black dude. We walking far enough."

"She tell you to come now?"

"She ain't say shit."

"So why we going?"

"You gonna trick tonight?"

"Yea maybe. I really want to get stoned."

"You gonna fake it?"

"Yeah I tie him off first. Maybe don't even gotta fuck him. Fake suck him off a little," Sienna tells her gal pal as she holds her fist to her mouth, spits into the fist and fakes a fist-blowjob in the air, "I like it like that. I like the ones that sweated all day. Then he passes out and I rip him off. Ya, tonight I think."

"You wanna move out huh?"

"Can't go nowhere here. I want to hustle, ya know? Can't hustle nothing worthwhile here."

"In the city, huh?"

"Yeah. Maybe. I don't know. I still have to pee."

Sienna shuffles herself around a dry white branch bush sprouting from the garbage glittered desert sand. Her hair glows like sterling steel in the moonlight. The roadside is vast and empty between the tennis court condos and the aluminum paneled homes. Innovation can be found in the tightest of needs. When Kim was a virgin, and the boys wanted to fuck, she used her backdoor to keep good friends. Here they use sliding glass patio doors for their main entrance and shitty pressed wood doors with replaceable key doorknobs for their yard door. Sienna pisses. Kim's getting anxious, "I don't like this road no more." Sienna un-squats and the double Desert Kats continue on to find the Four Room hotel.

"I gonna dye my pubs red and blue," Kim says before looking both ways into the darkness of the multi miles long desert road. "Come on," she says pulling on Sienna's fingers to cross the road to the sidewalk side. She's fully chipped away all her nail polish by this time. She used to bite her nails. The meth has changed that habit. The grinding of her molars will suffice, and a chip, chip, chip away at her polish. Sienna did not have braces. She may have benefited from braces. Now at nineteen her crooked grinding, stained teeth are a most alluring feature to those looking to pay bottom shelf with a nice label. She breaks her heel crossing the street. "Fuck those skank shoes," Kim squawks from the curb. The bulimic silver haired, purple eye shadowed, white lip-stick Desert Kitty is fumbling around trying to put the heel back on. A car is coming. She flips it off as it soars past and hobbles to the curb. She sits her free-flowing, for a price, ass on the curb and plays with the heel dangling from a single staple. "You had those new 5-hours they got at 98 plus?"

"What?"

"Energy drink?"

"No."

"You just stole those heels, right?"

"Cheap shit. Can't steal nothing good out here, cause there ain't just nuthin' good." Kim's really over her friend's whimpering, grabs the shoe, tears the heel right off, tosses the wooden peg into the street. The heel bounces and falls diagonally across the double yellow line. "Yer a princess. Gimme the other one," she squeals as her flakey skinned knuckle gnarled hand goes for Sienna's good heel shoe. "I can do it," Sienna snaps back swatting the nasty hand away, "You need lotion," and slips off her own shoe, gently snaps the heel like a lady and places it in the gutter. Nicely. Leans it against the curb. The wind blows the heel down. "Come on," Kim complains as she grabs hold of her inner elbow and lifts her from the pavement, "I wanna get stoned."

*

Whap, Whap, Whap. Kim slaps her palm against the sliding door of the metal trailer made "house" in the back of the Four Rooms hotel. The minuscule yaps from a Chihuahua scampering towards the glass door startles the team. Yap, Yap. Yap. The Chihuahua taps its paws along the inside of the glass. Now there are two. Why are there two? Yap-Yap / Yap-Yap. What the fuck. Kim squats to doggy level. Taps back at the dogs. "You had to kill yer dog, didn't ya?" Sienna asks her.

"Yeah. She had tongue tumor. Filled up her whole mouth. She could breath and all, but I shot her."

"You bury her?"

"Up on that lot past the Entra Road," Kim looks into the glass, "Where is she?"

Yap –Yap-Yap—

　　　　　　Yap –Yap-Yap—

　　　　　　　　　　　　Yap –Yap-Yap—

From behind the glass the owner approaches, scolds the tiny mutts, "Shut up, stupids," and kicks the leader, slides the door open, the pups rush out yapping at the girl's heals, "What you hoe's want?"

*

Billy-Sue is pear shaped fat, twisted, with a wandering eye, loose toothed, dry leathered desert skin, three chins, who wears three different flower print blouses, talks in a raspy two packs a day cigarette voice, and a consistent nose bleed of a methhead who immediately inquires, "Carmalita ain't wit you?" and she peeks out past the sluts, "Can't trust her. Thief. She steal everything. Steal your baby's virginity if you leave her with the stroller," and she looks Kim right in the eye while her other eye stares off into the night, "She ain't waiting in a car out there or something?"

"Nah, chill Sue, skank ain't walking with us no mo."

"That true?" Billy-Sue asks Sienna, "You trust worthy. I like you. Pretty, proper...not like this cunt. She telling me the truth?"

"Yeah, yeah. She ain't wit us no more."

"Okay. You good?"

"Yup."

"Bet you make more money if you got some braces," then turns to Kim, "You need some weed?" and invites them both in, shooing the dogs away with a kick to the head, "Just kick them. They can take it. Idiots."

"What's wrong with them?"

"They're retarded. You retarded or something?

"Huh?"

"Nah, they ain't. My cousin's like that. It ain't right callin' them retarded."

"I didn't."

"I know sweet-pea, I said it. I calling myself out. I'm a piece of shit, but hey, God didn't make Adam perfect. That prick hit that shit the first shot Eve gave him. Come on, I smoke you out."

*

The girls didn't stay more than two or three minutes after sucking down a half a blunt left over from Billy-Sue's black boyfriend. BS couldn't stop talking about the massive dick the guy had and how she ain't never fucked a black guy with a purple hard on before 'til DHS got ghetto and she started listening to Tupac when her daughter was back in Junior High. Kim just couldn't listen to it anymore. She'd fucked Billy-Sue's guy like six or seven times in the past month; paid for it too. It ain't all that purple. And it ain't all that big. She gave him rebates and shit cause he liked to tell her he loved her. That he was gonna be her ticket to a real club in Compton. Full nude. All cash. All black guys. Kim liked black guys. She just didn't tell a nobody that. "I ain't listen to your racist ball talk. We outty. But I wanna buy an eighth from ya next time yer boyfriend pays for ass lick. He like that you know. You should try it," Kim calls it all out, in jest.

Billy-Sue laughs.

Billy-Sue knew he liked that. She liked it too. She liked blowing on the bunghole and snorting bumps off his black balls while he got high. He had left the half a blunt the last time she gave him the Dirty Desert Sanchez. Kim knew all that too. Kim just didn't know what he got outta Billy-Sue's, ya know, body type? Maybe Billy-Sue got money? Like bank money? Inheritance? Cash it was not. Last time she brought him down here when BS was Costco-ing, she knocked him silly, snooped around, found the cookie jar, $300 bucks in fives and dollars; bitch broke like us.

Its dark out. Still too early to work. Should get jobs in Cathedral City, strip until real dark, then bang out a couple hundies for a flip in the sack.

"I ain't ever leavin," prideful as she ain't, Kim still let Sienna know.

"I know. This our home."

"Ain't no home. Shit's the devil's butthole, but I like the devil."

"You would."

"I ever tell you 'bout when I met that Satanist from Rancho Mirage?"

"You let him bleed on you."

"I let him bleed into my pussy."

"That's fucking nasty."

"I ain't do it for free. He said he'd have six demons protect me forever if I did it."

"His dick was bleeding?"

"Nah. That shit's gross, nineties freaky shit. Nah, he cut his wrist like this," and Kim slices her down her wrist.

"That's how you kill yourself," Sienna says blushing. She knows. She messed up the first time. The nurse was an idiot. Told her, "You have to cut up and down if you really want to kill yourself dear." Sienna did it right the next time, but it was in the restroom, back of the Sidewinder Café. She was found pretty quick and people had to stop dowsing their pancakes with maple syrup so they could rubberneck as the paramedics dragged a kicking and screaming silver haired banshee named Sienna out of the bathroom at 7am. She was all strung out. She was over all those, "Fucking jealous faggots who can't pay up for limp dick!"

Fuck it. Die instead. 7am seemed like a good time to die.

"You would know."

"Yeah. I guess I would."

And they laughed. And they continued back to the main strip

of their desolated desert town. And there were a lot of stars out that night, but then again when isn't there. They had fun being girls. They figured 22 would be a good day to die.

Maybe they'll fuck that night.

Maybe they'll even get stoned again,

but then what?

The weed makes them giggle not cry.

Shit.

The girls like the night now. They like their town. Shit ain't so bad. They don't mind being scum. Mom ain't no college graduate.

The Desert Kats like the smoke screen best of all.

#18
INdecent
PROposal

The bud was fucking huge. He could hardly believe it. Jake had been on a cleanse for weeks now. No weed. No sugar. No dairy— Nothing —just water and bottles of kombucha. That was over now. Three weeks in Portland. Six dips in the forest's mineral hot springs. They used bleach to clean the tubs. Now he has returned to Southern California, to die. He'll croak later, today it was time to feast, only after getting stoned as fuck. "How much you want for it?" Jake asked his dealer. "Not for sale brother," replied the off-the-grid Burbank druggist of green. "Everything's for sale. How much?" Jake tries again. "Not. For. Sale," he is told. Jake has to think about this. The bud can't be smaller than three feet long. Sure there's a massive stem in the belly of this beast of delicious green natural candy, but it's all one piece. The stems are thin and the leafy buds have intertwined their transparent hairs so much that you could never decipher where one ends and another begins. It is all one big bud.

"$500?" Jake offers.

"Not for sale," says the dealer.

"Eight"—

"Nope"—

"Twelve Hundred"—

"Not going to happen man"—

"Sixteen Hundred. That's my final offer," Jake says and waits, patiently.

*

The dealer didn't answer.

It was clear— There was going to be no sale —Jake was not satisfied.

*

This Jake was cut from a very different cloth than his green-collar distributor. Jake spent his LA days rolling through Hollywood in his jet-black B, M, Double-U. He could have bought a medical marijuana card years ago by now, but that wouldn't be cool. Cool was to buy from a local dealer. Cool was living in Malibu and sitting in rush hour traffic for two hours on the 101 to have his "readers" do notes on scripts he was supposed to read. That's how Jake-the-Make figured it. That's what a gangster rapper would do to score his weed while he lived the good life in his beach side crib. Dre didn't buy no weed, from no fake Rite-Aid. Hells no. Dre got his stuff from the street. Jake, himself, was as black as a white panther and bleached to even better resemble freshly fallen snow, so he can tan more. He didn't come from rags either. Jake-the-Make was born in Beverly Hills, Bel Air adjacent. The boy was born with a credit card tattooed into his finger prints and an inheritance he'd kill for if his parents weren't so financially hospitable to him already. He listens to The Chronic like his Pops listened to Blood Sweat and Tears, and his Grandpa listened to Dizzy— Classic Hip Hop all the way, Jake would say. This was his third BMW. First one was white and donated from his father's collection for his sixteenth birthday. The second one Jake got for college and was blue.

Jake's Mom got him this new black one when he made Executive after selling his friend's reality show. Jake's friend is quite the basketball star turned male rapist. Outed. The coach and the league called it a set up. Jake knew his boy had roofied the Beverly High basketball jock and popped his cherry. Jake didn't judge. Gay is gay and money is what money does. Now they had a TV show and Jake had a new BMW.

Fucker was old already. Twenty-Six didn't look good on a young executive producer these days. He could feel it; someday soon his colleagues would notice the wrinkles along his knuckles. Jake figured he only had a few more months to lock down some celebrity actress sugar-mama before the folks cut him off. Maybe there was a surgery for knuckle wrinkles? What would Dad do? That's what he always asked himself. What would Daddy do? What would Poppa Banks offer this guy for this massive marijuana bud of envy that he can show off to the script readers and assistants.

"Okay. How about a couple passes to Deja Vu?"—"Passes to a strip club? Really?"—"I know one of the girls. She'll give you free time in the back. Might even blow ya"—"Not for sale bro"—"I have a brick of coke at the house?"—Silence—"Fine. Forget the lap dances and blow, I have something better"—the dealer was all ears although he would never budge on this point—"A few of us at the studio get these really high-class girls, ya know? I get you like two, on me, and how 'bout you give me the bud?"—"Pass"—"You gay?"—"Not a chance"—"You want my car or something?"—The dealer just shakes his head—"Man, come on. Everybody has a price. What is it?"—Jake was not used to not getting his way—"Your grandma need to make her mortgage or something? Maybe you have a sick Aunt? Your girlfriend want tits? How about a yearlong membership to a waxing salon for your favorite girl? You like 'em like a baby, I can tell."—"Nope, my grandma's dead. No aunts. And I'm not buying none of my girlfriends fake boobs or fucking children"—"A tranny with a supply of Viagra?"—"Go to hell."

This guy had Jake sweating. Jake didn't break a sweat. Jake bought everything he had ever wanted. He'd already traded up girlfriends with the bait of fur coats in LA. "But isn't it too hot for fur," she had asked. "Not in the Alps," he had charmed her and then flew her to the mountains and said it was the coke that had prevented him from getting hard, so he promised to buy her a car when they got back to the states.

This dealer was not going to go for that. Besides, the Alps were too classy to take a drug dealer from the Burbank— Maybe a meal at BJs and a round of video games—"You like video games?" Jake asks him. "Not so much," the dealer replies without a beat. "Gambling? You want to go to Vegas? I'll set you up big. Got girls there too"—"Don't like Vegas since they got rid of the coin drops"—"Jesus Christ, man. What the fuck do you want for it?"—"Nothing"—And Jake stomped his foot, paced around, whimpered like a caged dog, and nearly scratched his eyebrows off from all the spoiled rotten stress. "You're going to regret this. I'm gonna leave. I'm gonna buy this dime bag off ya and leave and tomorrow you'll wake up and your car won't start, or you'll find a lump on your balls, or…Fuck it— I'm just going to curse you and everything about your fucking life and then you'll wish you had sold me your stupid bud," Jake ranted, tossed a ten-dollar bill on the table, took the tiny baggy, and left saying, "You lost a client."

The dealer shrugs as the door closes behind Jake. Another dude shows up. "How you doing, man?" the new dude asks. "I'm cool," says the dealer. "Shit, that is one Big Ass Bud! You want to smoke that?"—And that's when the dealer said, "Sure," and together the two men enjoyed the weed without a price, save for friendship, and the mutual respect for the green ass bud.

#19
HABIT
UAL
mythos

From her belly grew three massive tentacles. The appendages were muscular flesh that would reach into the night sky; their clubs were functional vaginal lips and passages that could collect stars from the dark matter of space and time. These frontal tails were extensions to her arms and legs; they were her perfection. If you were to be hers, she would wrap herself around your flesh, spiraling along your mass, suckling your extremities with her luscious vaginal clubs.

Throughout the day the sheness would relax her fleshy feminine appendages and sprawl herself out along the sea. The ocean's salty water bathed her in acres of saliva and the sweat of an infinite number of men lost at sea, stranded on the shallow shores of empty islands populated by soulless sexual fantasies. The current would spread her hair like a fan of needle thin serpents. A head spawning a billion appendages that would pick at the deceased sea men who had swam out to a loveless suicide. Unfortunately, the flesh of death lacks nutrition. The death of these men had corrupted their protein and her sheness might as well have been grinding sand kernels between her molars. The tiny male brail had always left her stomach hollow and cramped, causing her mind to cringe from the pressure of the sea. By midnight she'd grow restless and maturate her three appendages to extend into the nightscape so she may catch burning stars with her sex lips and toss them toward the myriad of moons orbiting this disproportionate living sphere.

Fish of a thousand kinds would spin schools of tornados to the rhythms of her humming. Throughout the days she has grown fonder of using her throat to tame her own melancholy as she waded through this sudden flesh-station her essence had accumulated from, from the minerals of the deep, like the civilization of a bazillion cells embraced to hold the form of a jellyfish. Was she ever in search of a mate or was the fire on the mainland keeping her timid and cowardice because the ocean was cool and ever flowing despite being caged within the confines of its surrounding soil, the continents' walls of granite, and her father's promises.

*   *   *

Flutters of winged lions with peacock tails would circle over herness, land upon her belly for rest, soar away, only to return to circle her once more. They were on the hunt for whale meat, not women birthed from gods. Some of the soaring kings of the wild would roar while others would purr and tumble in the playfulness of heaven's clouds. And her sex was warm and wet and wiser none-the-less of hisness, the giant that stood upon the continent. She would avoid him forever. That was her father's single request. He would insist she never find him on the land, sky, or sea. Her glory was too great for even a father to part with, but her stagnation in the Sea would be the end of his light if ever a cult of mosquitos nested and reproduced within her tied umbilical. Fathers are precarious.

Her father, who had been born from the wombs of sixteen prepubescent gods and his single elderly father, the god of indignation, allowed her to live upon a chosen sphere as she wished. Her wish was that of entitlement based on the maddening sense that her soul was being drawn out of her essence and that she was certain to pain herself as does a swordfish who thrashes when caught on a fisherman's fork. Her father, in turn, made gloriously shallow commitments that the upright beasts of the world she was to rest with would admire the sight of her mystical flesh reclined in the waves of the sea, and sacrifice themselves for her. The sea was the only real estate large enough to facilitate her immense size, being that she was the last daughter of a god, her ego was more than a reflection of her birthright. And in return she would ignore the fisherman. The ocean assisted in this futile commitment. That is the promise she was sure she could not hold. That was the promise that gave her credence and allowed her the patience to toil alone as she intentionally avoided the statue of the giant on the mainland forever. A lie. Float. Remain. Forgetful. Yearning. Strong. Weakened. Tempered. Bored. Careless. Drifting. The freedom granted from being bound in chastity chains adrift a sea of inconsistency was the under-toe, tidal waves, whirlpools, and hunger amongst the flesh eating, water winged, gilled beasts who would feast upon themselves in their specie's sacrifice for survival and the rape of extinction, is the freedom that distracted her sense of past and future. And the electrified eels of the sea caves would tend to her needs by suckling her backside to pick the barnacles from her skin. She may have cried for the honey bees that washed ashore weekly if she had ever known a bee to be so full of life, but as far as she could recall, the soaring pollen seekers had just kept leaping to their death in the salted sea with no hope for sugar and sweets. And the bees were a reminder that she had never stopped avoiding him on the land.

*

The giant's feet were as firmly planted into the estate as the stone they were carved from. His arms were the mass of a redwood's base, the bark stretched like leather, his veins raised and pulsating with a fever for the sea. He had been the giant that had set fires to the dry brush across all eighty-nine continents. Smoke billowed from each pile of charcoaled debris as the muscle and bone of the sphere's inhabitants sacrificed their lambs, their kids, their fawn, and their fables in order to understand the treachery of the now still giant who stands naked, tall, and silent, doing nothing, but burning down his land. More than two thirds of this world labeled him the horror of a monster's fear. The remaining population believed him to be a recluse from his own kind. These inhabitants prayed for his revelation. They called up the gods who commanded the gods of the final gods who sacrificed their godliness for complete knowledge and truth of the Universe and its Opposite. They asked these gods to reveal the lover in the sea to him. If he mates, he may not flame the fires on us, was what they believed.

His gods were the women who birthed him. He was not a child of a single coupling. He was as if he was her own father, yet born a son not a god. His stomach wore the mark of miracles and mysteries. This giant of the land had three navels birthed from three women. The mothers were open wounds of cosmic dark matter completed with the seed of the suns. With every night came the fear of the day. With every day came the retreat of his mothers around his crown. Three wombs collected to balance the wake of the moons that by midnight would tilt and twirl the sea-water into unconsciousness— her dream. By day the blinding truth was as fierce a flame to his naked eyes as the stars she collected without a spark of pain along her appendages smacking their blood filled vaginal lips in the cold. And his phallus was a pillar of carnis as he stood staring blindly over the crumbling beach walls out to the vast bath of amniotic waters where she waded bare, her hair freely a drift, untangled from the undercurrent.

*

The earths and the fifty massive dying spheres that orbited the sea and the land, had created a familial atmosphere within her orifices. Into her ears swam the reborn plankton that were regurgitated from the narwhales that in turn would penetrate her arteries with their spiraled tusks filling her heart with a numbing chorus of the orgasms sung by illustrious narwhales mating with aquatic pachyderms. Her anus would excrete, by the hundreds, heavy minuet eggs of pearl all packaged in a fine silk membrane.

Rabid sharks would launch themselves from their lazy depths to tear at the egg casing. When ingested in large doses, these eggs would induce a psychedelic jaunt for the flesh-eating sharks. And the fish would grow arms, and the sharks would grow legs, and their phallus would stand tall and erect and still they would devour each other in a fashion damaging to a cannibal's integrity.

Bottom dwelling clams, the size of bears, would unbury themselves from the sandy seabed to swallow the very eggs she disclaimed for the world to reprocess. And he would watch from the shore as the waves rushed against her closed and shackled uterus. Her pubic hairs were not free. An illusion from the seaweed caught along her chains. Her pelvis had been welded shut. Closed. Not for entry. Only when she deposited her eggs of lifelessness would a small door open from the rear of her metal diaper.

*   *   *

The giant's multiple mothers' burned a crown along his forehead scorching the green leafed curls of his wild flower hair. He was sedated. His feet were heavy. Night would fall.

He would wait no longer. He had chosen a path so simple. He would crush the cities and enter the sea. His steps would be slow. Each foot will demolish hundreds of homes and offices. He would enter the sea and trudge along the base of the ocean and rape the buoyant flesh that floats before his eyes.

It was futile to avoid him if he was going to be so bold as to splash through her home with such a steady step and shine to his naked eye. There was more to him than the bulk of his flowing blood. This was the everything she was banned from accepting into herself. If he even spoke one word, the meaning would span a lifetime. And if he could find a way to enter her, to stay inside as she struggled and moaned, then she would surely defy her god, her father.

Why not?

Why not entice the giant and see how militant he is to have her? Even if she gave herself to him, he would still have the satisfaction of rape by defiling a god's daughter. She would ease her bellies appendages along his neck and shoulders when the aqueous sap rises from his pores. Her elongated tentacles will perform the acts of desire with the strength of a celestial army. Armies of gods and angels, demons and mercenaries who have fought for the placement of lands and oceans along the void of dark matter. They would battle with swords and tear the flesh from each other's spines with their molars and claws. The sphere on which he and she resided was the closest planet to the three mother suns; it was a past battleground basting in the blazing embers of the universe's dying daughters.

*

The time was always the middle of the night when the sea would temporarily fill with the glow of his crown. She would turn her back on the night sky and instead watch the holocaust of his mother's suns extinguished under the sea. His heavy soles would push the bottom dwelling clams that had claimed her eggs deeper into the sand of the sap soaked earth with every step closer to her, he would take.

Treasures saved the pollen of his flowered leaf hair. Pollen absorbed through the veins of the leaves would travel throughout his carnis body to his coupled pebbles. His dangling stones had the potential of expelling diamonds from his hardened phallus. These transparent gems were known to shave the most impenetrable of metals. His expulsion was the seamen of the alchemist's gods; salient, acute metaphysical diamonds enchanted with the gyration of a hundred quaking planet's cores that would violently carve at the chains of chastity to give her the single choice to reveal her rabbet, her father's diamond in the rough, her laceration and within her soul, the yeast that makes the giant rise.

*

Her fantasies in space were as transparent as the lies she perpetrated to herself to find a way to a celestial earth of matter. Her father had planted this daughter a garden of sulfur. A landscape where succulent living, the consciousness of tubeworms, once gave purpose to mammalian souls. Now this soup had become a warm bed of penetrable scent for his daughter to grow the soft flesh around her enlightened dark matter of essence. And the flesh would be sealed by a soothing membrane of suede and the essence would harden into bone and soon enough in years to come she would sprout the appendages from her belly to play with the stars to tease and tantalize the terra firma until he came into her sea.

*

The smaller fish would scatter as he stepped closer and closer to her drifting wake. The gentle movement of her fingers spread the variety of tides across the globe. The massive toothed, leather skinned octopods would, without trepidation, lunge themselves toward him. Curling their parasitic sucker infested tentacles around his entirety. His orifices were subjects to the rape of the single fingered appendages blasting from a single breast, loose flesh, a breast that can hold no shape, and a nipple expulsing air bubbles. His nose would be clogged. His ears stuffed. Two or three of these Octopi's elongated arms would push their way into his mouth. His anus. His urethra. The others would squeeze his thighs, his claves, both his wrists, and his hands would try to contain a flow of blood. The Octopi's tentacles would tie around his bicep, choke his throat, and suckle on his eyeballs. The mouths of the Octopods were only the vaginal comparison to the desperate pussy-cat in heat which screams in agony upon penetration. Smacking their lips together the Octopi attack. Salivating in the already salty sea, which burns their passing ovaries like severed arteries gushing red oil slicks, they would bruise his skin and gnaw upon his hair. If they had teeth they could break his surface and suck him dry. Blood that would surely fill their breasts so they may rise to the surface of the waves like she had and grow to mate on land with the monkeys in the trees and the rodents in the sand— If he hadn't severed theses parasitic Octopi knots from his discomfort and released their meaty breast heads out to sea, then he may have never returned to the waters for a second time, this being his ninth.

*   *   *

The black and red ink stained water from the torn muscle and fat of the estranged Octopods paints a darkness in the ocean, another mask to peak her interest and allow herself to drift closer into his path. Just for show. The current crashes white water against her breasts. Her belly turns south again. She sees his helicoid eyes of indulgence, spiraling in, the vacuum of everything and nothing with the spice of rebellion and humor about both of their finite pasts and infinite futures.

The moon will shift. Forced to the East off the Z axis. The Mothers of the Universe, the dark matter, have collected the mass of all life. The tide has turned. The sporadic air bubbles have grown heavy and hard. Stones— Thousands of bulleted pebbles —Fragments of sand cascade against her suede skin. The Mothers are angry. Bruised again and again. The dark matter has had its patience with the Sea— No more. And the grains of sand, the trillions of stones, the monstrous rocks that bite and poison the under flesh? They will penetrate her amphibian spirit, drawing question to her innocent mind, and immaculately rape her in the sea and force her to bare billions of still-born crustaceans that drift to the continents and seed the forests after traveling upstream in the bellies of salmon, dropped in the mating ponds, and sprouting as the vegetation of smoke for the natives, the last of the risen people.

Those of the industrialized and tragically civilized masses had been cast out from their burials upon his absence on the soil at midnight. The now broken peoples of the cities were as quick to repentance as he was wise to abandon them and lug his mass of dirt and soil through the sea to reason with passion and devour the fragrance of the sulfur gas, temporarily satisfying his cannibalistic salacity until he could lick the inside of her flesh and she could ingest his children.

*

The dark matter above the invisible skyline ceased to blanket her every inhibition. Her father patiently sat upon his godly throne of gas anticipating a time to battle against the giant that so thoughtlessly came to poison his kin with diamonds and then distribute her pearls. Her parents just did not know where she had gone to. The stones that had buried her alive and attempted to smother her new friendship, had all sunk to the sea floor, melting into a majestic coral reef mapped with the living sphere's molten lava that would ooze from its core and slither through the valleys of the uncharted reef. And once again she would lower herself into the cloaked darkness of the depths to be with him.

Her carnis would augment into a lavish skin, softer to the touch than the suede that he had imagined her essence to be sealed in. He would act unaware. She herself was surprised by her willful metamorphosis. Her shackles still remained. Is it she that is this thin membrane that now drapes over his skull in the manner of a mystic entering a session of mesmerizing prayer? He would twist his forearms into her. Use his calloused fingers to twirl her thin sheet of a form into his grip and he would tug her close and she would cloak him with her absoluteness and yet still avoid the vacuum of this giant skeptic's helicoidally animated eyes. The membrane, which would be her hand, would flutter and stroke his phallus, washing the waters around his dangling stones and in time set off a series of penetrating diamond ejaculate against the metal shield that guarded her canal, her passage; his time capsule.

And again, and again he would bombard her father's gated compound with his circus of shredding seamen. The darkness of the ocean blasted away into a shine by the sparks and fragmental streaks of electricity ricocheting from the striking diamonds against the metallic casing. The jolts of electrons would pierce her nerve endings, peddle to the metal along the nervous interstate, in and up the overpass of her breasts, nearly escaping from the opening atop her nipples, but instead curving along the esophagus and penetrating her spine so the electrocution could galvanize her neurotransmitters into submission and give him an ample chance at seducing her past, her initial rape of his initial intention.

Was she struggling? Absolutely.
Was he brutal? Yes.

His brutality played out with a creative care as he gnawed her flesh during the inflammation of her membrane that again was flowering with flesh, muscle, breasts, lips, fingers, and soon enough he will, with a final wrenching of the shaved metal, contest to remove the belt of subtle virginity, penetrate her father's glory, and drown their sorrows, thrashing through the sea, murdering eels, captivating bottom dwellers stoned on shells, bewildering their animation of spirit, tickling their souls, bloodletting their tongues into each other's mouths, and awaiting the diamonds to shave the lining of her tunnel to bare the eighty-eight children to dine upon and serve as fragments to the Natives, only to awaken the next morning, once again her sheness floating aimlessly in the sea, and hisness, stone cold, back on land, as stationary as an illicit idol surrounded by the fauna that has risen and walked from the sea while the medicinal flora sprouted from her pearls now washed ashore into the earth of his pedestal. And the scent of the flora would remind him of a catastrophic event that has him uprooting his stoned soles so he may gallivant into her ocean— night after night —to wade through the sex of the sea, she.

And with the remnants of the salt he's left between her thighs, she would bake the grains and melt them with the heat of the suns enabling her to inhale his majestic opiate as he exhaled her sensational cannabinoids— This was their dream of how nothing came to be. This is the Mythos of what you need not know. This is the truth. This is.

This.

4# 20(s)

FOUR-

TWENTIES

First—

Kelly had to call Jake. Jake had to call Candy. And Candy called Jill. Janet heard about it from Joanie, who found out from Brady. Brady had been eating Jill out when he heard Candy say over the mobile speaker, "Dude like countdown to 4/20. We're going to Frisco, you in?" Shortly after Jill had finished Brady off, he returned the favor by skating his way through the Santa Rosa residential track homes to his girlfriend Toni's house to break up with her. Toni wasn't home. Her older sister Janet answered the door. Brady always liked Janet, "You wanna go to Frisco for 4/20?" he asked her, invited her, bummed a ride from her, hopefully will sleep with her by 4:20 on 4/20 instead of Jill again. "How old are you?" Janet asked him. "Eighteen," he said, "I got my med card. I'm good. Want to get high?"

"I'm twenty," she said, "Duh, I want to get high."

Second—

Washington Square Park was filled by 10am. Who knew stoners could wake and bake so early? These potheads had come from Brooklyn, Upstate, Alabama, the Carolinas; accompanied by bridge and tunnel with Rolling Rocks in their hands and blunts rolled. Carmen had hoofed it from Union Square— 12 Blocks —past the dread head, black, busted pixie on the corner of 8th and University who, on a loop, cackles her little lost hen pitch, "Extra dollar, extra quarter—Hello!" Carmen was meeting up with Louie and Stan. They were slow to buy during the rush and now they were panicked. "I'm doing ounces at $420 today," she says looking over Louie's shoulder at the collection of crystal crackhead transplants from Detroit who are unilaterally sniping for half/quarter cigarettes that have been dropped to the earth after the cancer collector got lectured by some castrated hippy in yoga gear sporting their medicinal marijuana patch on their forearm. 4/20 was going off this year with colors of drugs and spectaculars. The gays are collecting as well. Gay Ganja Guys with signs. "Dude that's way too high. We got like $300 for an ounce," Louie tries to score Carmen's undivided attention. "Four Twenty," she says flashing her eyes back at him only to look left and wave over one of her pals. "What up creepster?" and she hugs into a big African American Rasta woven in Jamaican gear, "You always beautiful girl," he says and nods to Louie. Carmen asks, "Where's RZA?" — "Home stoned baby girl," and a kiss on the cheek and smoking and toking and he struts away into the mass that has filled NYC's Downtown Arches in the heart of NYU.

Third—

They had all met in the heart of the Alabaman Strawberry Field, "It's a short season, but perfect fer four twenty— You got the acid?" the mullet head asked the long-haired confederate-ly bikinied blonde; she bleached it, used to be pink, before that blue, sometime in high school she had that shit jet-black and ICP clown faced look, but she was ginger down there— What of it? "Yeah, I got et," she said as she slid the dime bag out from her freckled right breast cup; four squares totally blank and soaked in pure acid from St. Louis.

He lit the pre-Four Twenty, Four Twenty blunt and they gave each other their tab. She sucked his dirty index. He had been working in the cow shed in the am. Pop gave him the day off to get his dick wet in that sweet neighbor's cousin— This girl right here. "We gonna cum at four twenty?" he asked. She cocked her head, "Not without weed between my legs, and a big black blunt in my lips."

Four—

It's on the 4th floor, dude— Apartment 20 —obviously. Don't push. Chill man. This elevator is slow as fuck. I get it. What am I supposed to do? Yeah, I see them. There's gonna be like four groups of twenty. I told you. Yes. Dude, you stoned? Yeah. Well I'm stoned, but I'm not retarded— You. You're retarded— (sigh)—I know your third cousin, forth removed is retarded. Yes. I know it's your sister's favorite story. You have an incestuous family. What's new? You're from California. Oh. Excuse me. Long Beach. Does that really make it any better? Not redneck or hippy. Okay, just crazy. Rich? Very funny. You're not that rich. Your cousin was? Look, two more. Total potheads—Yeah, so? I'm a functional pothead. There's a difference. No. Well, yeah, every day. All day. Yes. About $60 a week or less. Now I'm vaping. No not today. Today's 4/20. I'll smoke weed today again. Well I never stopped smoking weed— That would be crazy. Look skaters. One, two. Seven. Twelve. Shit that's a lot o' skaters. Shit-vator's here. We all gonna die in here before we get to 420-ville? How many of us are in here? One, Two, Three. Fuck you I lost count. Twelve, thirteen, fourteen— Ding —4th floor! Move it.

First Continued—

Janet forced Brady to go to the spot and pick up for them. He got a couple top-shelf pre-rolls, a quarter of mid-range Indica for the J, and for himself a quarter of top-shelf Indica and cashed in some points for a quarter of bottom shelf Sativa shake and two house-rolls. They were both zooted by the time Brady's girlfriend, Janet's younger sister, came home and found them necking. She couldn't take her eyes off Janet's hand tugging on Brady like she was milking a cow. Brady ignored Toni's childish girlfriend complaints, whines, accusations, and crimes. Janet tugged a little less. She waited for her sister to just leave already, "Leave!" Janet yelled at Toni the tiny tiger who was thrust into high-school heartbreak and hurt feelings, whorled onto her bed, a vortex of her innocent mind, untainted by the cheat, the dagger of confusion, and so young the thought should villainously arouse her, as she fingered herself, biting her lip, bleeding into the tears that soaked her pillow. She was on her knees. She was praying for the pain to go free. Confused and wondering why she'd be turned on by the burn of the porn show she saw and wanting to get high.

Second Continued—
    Stan's pissed that Louie let it come to this, "Dude I told you we needed to buy it earlier." There are massive clouds of smoke billowing all around the park. "We didn't have enough money. You should have smoked less this week," Louie tries to argue. "Who the fuck smokes less the week before 4/20. That's just whack man. You smoke more," Stan whines. "Then you should get a better job," Louie bitches. "You're a boner man. You don't even work," Stan slaps. "I'm on scholarship bro. I gotta keep up the grades. I ain't got time to study, smoke pot, and work," Louie rationalizes as Carmen lowers her 70s' auburn, silver sunglasses, lighting a cone and passing it to Stan. "So Lou, you buying it?"—"Yeah"—"I think that's a fabulous idea," she says and digs into her yarn weaved bag for the weed. Louie pulls out his wad of cash. He wants to count it. Not sure exactly how much he has. He withdrew $240. Stan got another $200. Did he give me his already? Yeah, he did. Is that too much, Louie? Louie is nervous. This is way too public. But it's okay, right? You can buy and sell weed in public today, right? And the crowd does a wave as they chant, "Four, Twenty! Four, Twenty! Four, Twenty!"

Third Continued—
    "I want to watch your dick get hard when we're peaking," Connie the Confederate said to her boyfriend. Mullet man nodded his head. He couldn't help smiling. He loved his girlfriend. They met in tenth grade; she passed him a note in homeroom that read, "I'll hold your Mullet when you

booze puke tonight. Then I'll suck your dick"—Now they're alone together in the strawberry field with psychedelia melting into their tongue pores. She scrapes both tabs off along her teeth and swallows. "Wanna get high?" he asks the only love in the only town he's ever known. "Sure," she replies. Pulls the tobacco rolled weed splif from his overall pocket, sparks it with the Zippo and a— Puff. Puff. Puff —The smoke rises and curls up along his embroidered plow and rifle trucker's hat. "You're beautiful," she says to him and takes the blunt; hits that shit.

Fourth Continued—

Whole place smells like weed. Dude that Pete Rock? Old skool tunes. Apartment 20 we go! We shouldn't have gotten on first man. We won't get in. No really. I swear man we should've let them all on before us. They only have 4 sets of 20 in the sesh. Hold up. Everyone's stopping. Dudes are going in. There better be some stoney chicks too man. I don't want a 4-20 sausage fest. Couple more then we're in mutha fucka. Oh, that door's rad. Looks like real pot. Open, weed door. Oh, she is fucking hot as shit. I'm Kevin. Sandra's a nice name. This way? What's the "D" tattoo on your chest about? Ha— We'll see. That's fucking hot bro. That pot bikini is hot. She don't care. She likes to be called hot. Fuckin' smiled at me. In there? Okay— Holy fuck, those chicks are twins. I mean, quadruplets, super-hot quadruplets? Their shirts spell out WEED. Dude, they spell fucking weed. Fucking—Weed. My dick is so hard I am going to pass out.

First Hit—

Kelly and Jake came over to Janet's. Brady rolled a blunt and packed a bong. Janet offered Kelly and Jake the first hit. They all got high. They started to fantasize about the coming 4/20. "Best Holiday, hands down," Jake said. "Best High-Holiday, ever," Janet replied. "You Jewish?" asked Brady. "No dude," Janet said punching him in the shoulder. Kelly takes another newly packed bong rip. Brady sparks a second blunt. Toni is in her room. She can smell the weed filling their parent's house. "They do know Mom and Dad are coming home after work, right?" she says to herself while realizing that if she doesn't get high with them then they get busted and not her. "Fuck I want to get high," she cries into her pillow.

Brady starts hooking up with Janet again. Kelly and Jake have no choice but to follow their lead. Toni still wants to get high. She has crept out of her bedroom door and down the stairs. Everyone is making out. Brady has his hand up Janet's shirt. Gross, Toni thinks. Kelly is actually blowing Jake by now. Hot, Toni thinks and swipes the half smoked blunt and heads to the yard. She lights up, gets fucking high, and returns to her freshly scented bedroom that does not reek of weed and takes a shower. Mom and Dad come home. Janet is 100% forbidden to go to the 4-20 celebration. Brady and the crew's parents will be informed by text about the happenings with their children and they too will be banned from attending any sort of 4-20 function tomorrow or forever. Toni however, will be free to hang with her friends outside of her sibling's prison…and secretly make a jaunt to the massive 4-20 festival and get super high with her real friends.

Second Hit—

Stan and Louie have scored their weed, but missed the hit of 4:20 on 4/20. "Fuck!" Stan cocks. "Hey chill man, it's four twenty," says some random stoner walking by without offering them a toke from his doobie. "You think Carmen ripped us off?" Louie asks Stan. "Yeah, duh?" Stan says turning his back on Louie moments before the Goddess of Green descended from the clouds of the netherworlds and into the palm of Louie the humbled. "I have sent you a gift of smoke through the vortex of my combater with your insect mind from the spore of the droplets that feather the earth into the soil blossom packed with a sweet nectar that is my essence and your epiphany of…" Without a conclusive thought, she vanished and Louie packed a chilin' and offered it to Stan and Stan smoked it, 4oo and 2o seconds after 4:20 on 4/20.

Third Hit—

The Confederate Bikini came off long ago. They were both completely covered in strawberry dye. Two white devils fucking the fields into a fire that clears the path for another crop. And he blew smoke inside of her. And she exhaled through her pours as she gasped the air filled with THC around her, as she chewed on the black tobacco stalk of weed in her mouth, and she came, and he blew more smoke into her as she sang with a twang on the fork of his uncrop-topped dang at 4:20.

Fourth Hit—
I can't. It's so hot. But all these dudes? And why can't we smoke too? Whatever I'm stoned. I like the way the second E girl shotguns her sister. She uses a little tongue. Twenty times. It's hot. Seven, Eight. These girls are going to be so fucking toasted after shot-gunnin' that shit. Oh my god they're touching each other. What the fuck. Kissing and smoking. What the fuck. I planned on getting high, but hell, Happy Four Twenty!